ALSO BY JENNIFER STURMAN

And Then Everything Unraveled

The Pact

The Jinx

The Key

The Hunt

And Then
I Found Out
the Truth

And Then I Found Out the Truth

Jennifer Sturman

Point

Library of Congress Cataloging-in-Publication Data

Sturman, Jennifer.
     And then I found out the truth / by Jennifer Sturman. — 1st ed.
       p. cm.
     Sequel to: And then everything unraveled.
     Summary: Although her environmentalist mother has been declared dead, Delia is sure that she is
still alive, but suspects that the father of the boy she likes is trying to make sure she does not stay
that way.
     ISBN 978-0-545-08724-7 (alk. paper)
     [1. Mystery and detective stories.   2. Missing persons — Fiction.   3. High schools — Fiction.
4. Schools — Fiction.]   I. Title.
     PZ7.S94125And 2010
     [Fic] — dc22

                                                                              2009040542

12 11 10 9 8 7 6 5 4 3 2 1   10 11 12 13 14 15/0

                                  Printed in the U.S.A.   23
                                  First edition, July 2010

                             Book design by Whitney Lyle

This book is dedicated to my mother,
Judith Heller Sturman

One

"Seriously?" said Natalie. "A forty-four?"

"I think it's pretty good," I said.

"Delia, in what universe does forty-four out of one hundred qualify as pretty good?" she asked as we left the physics lab and headed for the cafeteria.

"Forty-four is nearly half," I said. "So that means I got nearly half the answers right. Which is pretty good when you consider I don't remember taking the quiz."

Natalie tucked a strand of red hair behind one ear, perplexed. "Are you sure you weren't adopted? Or switched at birth? Statistically, it's highly improbable that such gifted people could produce a child so utterly lacking in scientific aptitude."

A glance in a mirror was enough to prove I was my parents' biological daughter: I had the standard-issue features of my mother's East Coast family but the coloring of my Indian father. Still, Natalie had a point. It was hard to explain how two Stanford PhDs — who'd even started their own Internet company — had ended up with me. "I guess I'm a genetic mutant," I said.

Natalie considered this with her usual gravity as we took our places in the lunch line. "A scientific black hole would be more accurate. Or differently gifted if you want to sugarcoat it."

"Um, thanks?" I handed her a tray and took one for myself.

Prescott Day School's resident chef was experimenting with theme-based cuisine, and I wasn't sure how I felt about it. Last week there'd been Macedonian Monday, which had meant a lot of lamb and yogurt, and today was Mongolian Monday, which also seemed to mean a lot of lamb and yogurt. We both asked for grilled cheese and found seats at an empty table against the cafeteria's far wall, where Natalie picked up right where she'd left off.

"Imagine how much better you'd have done if you'd paid attention to Dr. Penske in class," she said, cutting her sandwich into four precise triangles. "Or gone completely wild and — brace yourself, because this is a novel concept — but imagine what might have happened if you'd studied."

"I had other things on my mind," I said. "Important things."

"You managed to make plenty of time for Quinn Riley."

"I wouldn't call Quinn unimportant," I said, not even trying to control the uncontrollable smile that appeared on my face when I said Quinn's name.

Natalie didn't bother arguing about whether Quinn was or wasn't important — she knew how pointless that would be. She was also one of the few people who knew what I really meant by important things, like how my mother was hiding out from evil-doers in South America, and how I'd been busy trying to make it safe for her to come home. My dad died when I was thirteen, so I was already down to one parent — as far as I was concerned, ensuring that I didn't become a total orphan took precedence over homework.

Of course, if you'd told me in August that by September my mother would be in anonymous exile in Argentina and I'd be the newest member of Prescott's junior class here in Manhattan, I would never have believed it. I'd been blissfully clueless, enjoying the last days of summer back in California and entirely unaware that my life was about to unravel.

The whole mess started when T.K. — my mother's real name is Temperance Kittredge Truesdale, but since that's a ridiculous thing to call a person, she's always gone by T.K. — anyway, it all started when she organized a research trip to Antarctica. In addition to being an Internet tycoon, my mother's a huge supporter of environmental causes.

She'd told everyone the trip was to document the impact of global warming on polar ice shelves. But she'd also suspected that illegal oil exploration was under way in a part of Antarctica called the Ross Sea, and she'd wanted to see what she could find out. So she hired a small ship, posted online for volunteers to join her, and set off from Tierra del Fuego, at the southern tip of South America.

It turned out she was right about the illegal exploration. Unfortunately, she'd also inadvertently let the evildoers who intended to profit from the oil know she was on to them, and they'd hijacked her ship, the *Polar Star*, replacing the captain and crew and volunteer researchers with their own henchmen. The only legitimate person left on board besides T.K. was a climate change specialist from Australia. His name was Mark, and according to a psychic I knew, he was my mother's new boyfriend. I was less sure about that part, but either way the two of them figured out their shipmates were arranging for them to meet with foul play, and they escaped in the middle of the night in a Zodiac.

Amazingly, they managed to land unharmed in the wilds of Chilean Patagonia, and they'd trekked north from there to Santiago before sneaking across the Argentinean border and on to Buenos Aires. The idea was that they'd be safest in a large city, buffered by millions of strangers, and while Buenos Aires was thousands of miles from the Ross Sea, it was still the closest major commercial hub and the likely base of operations for anyone trying to accomplish something illicit in the region.

So that's where they were hiding out, though chances were good the evildoers thought they were dead. After all, the odds of normal people successfully navigating an ocean's worth of polar water in a rubber boat were pretty much zero. However, chances were also good that if the truth got out, the evildoers would want to remedy the situation. Which meant we needed to neutralize them before T.K. could come home and Mark could go back to Sydney or Melbourne or wherever.

All of which is a long way of saying that I'd had a lot to focus on besides physics lately. In fact, the last few weeks had been something of an emotional roller coaster, what with first having to worry about whether my mother was even alive — the hijackers faked the *Polar Star*'s disappearance, so just about everyone thought she was dead — and then trying to piece together what really happened.

And in case that hadn't been sufficiently chaotic, I'd also been uprooted from Palo Alto and sent to New York, where my mother's sisters, Patience and Charley (whose real name is Charity, because apparently my grandparents' baby name book predated indoor plumbing), were acting as my guardians. Now I was living with Charley while Patience handled any decisions about money or school.

I had to admit, it hadn't been all bad. Charley was slightly insane but in an interesting way, and Patience was completely uptight but she'd also be a useful person to have around in a crisis, like an alien invasion or monsoon. And though Prescott was a bit *Gossip Girl*, especially in comparison to West Palo Alto High, if Patience hadn't sent me here I'd never have met Natalie. And I didn't even want to consider the possibility of never having met Quinn, who came close to single-handedly canceling out all of the other turmoil and angst.

Anyhow, we were finishing up lunch and Natalie was

outlining a multistep plan to improve my academic performance — which was hopeless unless one of those steps involved magically downloading the contents of her brain into mine — when there was a buzzing in my book bag.

"You know you're not supposed to use your phone in school," Natalie said, not lifting her eyes from the piece of graph paper where she was sketching a timeline to go with the performance improvement plan.

I did know, but I also couldn't resist checking messages under the table — I was hoping for a text from Quinn. But the text was from Charley instead.

Mostly when Charley texted it was about dinner — she loves food as much as she loves clothes, and possibly more — but this was what she had to say today:

dr. p told me u flunked
starting 2nite no TV — all homework all time

I reread the message twice to make sure it really was from Charley and that she'd really meant to send it to me, but it was no mistake. She hadn't sent a follow-up text to apologize, either, even though it wasn't like *I* was the person in our two-person household who couldn't get through a single evening without some form of video entertainment.

For the first time since Dr. Penske had handed back the quiz with the "44" scrawled on top, I felt panic. I'd expected tough love from Natalie, but it hadn't occurred to me that Charley, who was as differently gifted as I was, wouldn't be sympathetic. And if this was Charley's reaction, I should probably be terrified of what Patience would do.

At least I could count on Quinn to understand. He'd help me figure out how to ward off Patience and steer Charley back onto the path of reason. And I'd see him when we had drama together at the end of the day, which meant I only had to make it through two more class periods.

Of course, every second of those two periods felt like it lasted a week, though thankfully neither Modern Western Civilizations nor precalc involved failing any more quizzes. And in spite of all the time I had to prepare, I was still overcome by a spasm of brain paralysis when I finally saw Quinn, leaning against the edge of the stage in the auditorium where our drama class met.

It wasn't just that he was a senior and godlike, with sand-colored hair and gray-green eyes that made me think of the Pacific on a cloudy morning. He also seemed to get me, and I thought I got him, too. It didn't even matter that we'd only known each other a few weeks, or that our single real date could have been construed as a research project, or that one of the two times he'd kissed me might not count since we'd been acting out the kissing scene from *Romeo and Juliet*.

Class started before my brain could unfreeze, so I didn't get a chance to really talk to him until after the bell rang and his minions had dispersed (Quinn didn't consciously collect people — they were just drawn to him by his general aura of undiluted cool). But then he walked me out of the auditorium and down the corridor and through the big front doors to the steps outside, where I poured out everything about my forty-four, and Dr. Penske calling my aunts, and Charley making bizarre threats, and Natalie's tough love, and how I had no idea what Patience might do but I feared carnage.

And when I was done, here's what Quinn said:

"Why are you taking advanced physics anyway?"

Which was more of a shock than Charley's text. I mean, there I was, expecting compassion and maybe even kissing (though probably not while we were surrounded by the entire Prescott student body in the process of leaving the building). But if anything, Quinn sounded like Natalie.

So without thinking I said, "Why are you taking AP calc?"

I regretted it as soon as the words were out of my mouth. Quinn was as bad at math as I was at science, and I already knew perfectly well he was only taking calculus because his father expected him to follow in his footsteps, which involved doing something complicated in finance — that is, when he wasn't potentially plotting with the evildoers who were the reason my mother was hiding out on another continent, though I wasn't sure about that part and, for obvious reasons, hadn't mentioned it to Quinn.

Quinn's lips tightened a bit at the edges, and for a moment his eyes looked more gray than green. But the moment ended almost before it began. "Point taken," he said, his tone easy.

"Sorry," I said lamely.

"Me, too. Let's forget it happened and go to the park. We can get you an ice cream and talk about what to say to your aunts."

Quinn and ice cream were two of my favorite things, so there was pretty much nothing I'd rather do. But I had an appointment I couldn't tell Quinn about since it had to do with figuring out whether his father was, in fact, in cahoots with evildoers. "I can't today," I said. "Maybe tomorrow?"

"Can't tomorrow," said Quinn. "I have a family thing. I guess we're logistically star-crossed, Juliet."

Sometimes Quinn calls me Juliet, because of how we had to do that scene together, and whenever he does it's good for another bout of brain paralysis. So all I could manage back was "Oh."

"But I'll talk to you later, okay?" he said.

I didn't even try to say anything else but just nodded, wondering as I did what would happen next. The steps had largely emptied out by then.

But before I could do much wondering, Quinn's lips were on mine.

And this time it definitely counted.

Two

The kissing left me giddy, and I practically skipped around the corner, to where I'd agreed to meet Rafe. I hadn't wanted everyone at Prescott to see that a thirty-something Colombian man would be escorting me home.

He was leaning against a parking meter, reading a copy of the *New York Post* and otherwise trying to look inconspicuous. When he saw me he folded the newspaper and tucked it under one arm. "Good afternoon, Delia," he said, his brown eyes warm behind little round glasses. "Did you have a nice day at school?"

Rafe's full name was Rafael Francisco Valenzuela Sáenz de Santamaría, and he was a private detective, though he dressed like a cross between an investment banker and a petting zoo attendant, in dark suits and silk ties patterned with small animals. Today it was white rabbits on a field of green twill.

I'd hired Rafe to help find T.K. soon after she disappeared, when everybody thought I was crazy for even suggesting she might not be dead. Actually, Quinn was the one who hired him, since I didn't have anywhere near enough money, though when Charley found out she insisted on paying Quinn back.

Based on the information I'd already gathered, Rafe was able to track T.K. down in South America. It had been a huge relief to confirm she was alive and well and that I wasn't an orphan, but until we could nail the bad guys who were out to get her, it wouldn't be safe for her to return home.

So now our investigation had entered its second phase, which was all about building a case against the evildoers so we could bring them down. And because T.K. wasn't the only person they seemed to be after — at least, not judging by how a black Range Rover had tried to run me over the previous week — Rafe was also supposed to be keeping an eye on me. Which was sort of comic, since he'd never have to worry about anyone confusing him with The Rock.

We took the subway down to Tribeca, to Charley's loft on Laight Street. Practically everyone at Prescott lived closer to school, in fancy doorman buildings or town houses on the Upper East Side. But that was how my mother and her sisters grew up, and Charley had been eager to put as much distance as possible between herself and her childhood without leaving Manhattan altogether.

Now she lived on the top floor of a converted nineteenth-century button factory, and though there was nobody to help with the door and the elevator didn't always work, once you did get upstairs you found yourself in the sort of relaxed, flowing space that didn't exist on Park Avenue. Except for the bedrooms and bathrooms, it was one vast room that could double as a roller rink, but mostly we used it for eating takeout and watching DVDs.

Charley arrived just as we did, so Rafe could finish the blushing and stammering that always happened when he first saw her while we were still in the elevator. Of course, Charley didn't even notice. This was partly because she was used to men adoring her — my aunt's ridiculously gorgeous, with long dark hair and luminous skin and amazing style, and she's also close to six feet tall — and partly because she was too busy talking.

"Look," she said to me, "your mom will never forgive me if your grade point average plummets on my watch, and I know I'm the last person to give anyone a hard time about anything requiring the slightest amount of left-brain dexterity, but you'd much rather have me giving you a hard time than Patty giving you a hard time, and the good news is that Dr. Penske reached me first and I somehow convinced him not to tell Patty, so we've dodged a bullet, but that's contingent on you doing a lot better on your next quiz, the date of which is supposed to be a surprise but I pried out of him it's going to be this Friday, so we'd better get cracking, and when I say we, I mean you and whomever we can find to help you. Rafe, can you do science?"

Charley tends to speak in run-on sentences. She's also the only person who calls Patience "Patty," not that Patience approves. Then again, Patience is the only person who calls Charley "Charity," so she's kind of asking for it.

"Wh-what?" said Rafe. It would've been pathetic if I didn't know how he felt. His blushing and stammering weren't that different from my brain paralysis.

"Science," said Charley. "Delia flunked her physics quiz."

That got Rafe's attention. "Flunked?" he repeated as the elevator doors slid open into the loft.

"Flunked is a strong word for it," I said. "I did get nearly half the answers right."

"Unacceptable," said Rafe. "What are we going to do?"

The use of the first-person plural seemed aggressive given that Charley was just my temporary guardian and Rafe wasn't any sort of guardian, but Charley was focusing on being severe. "We're going to start by spending every waking moment cramming physics into Delia's head until Delia is not only acing her class but is also ready to take first place in whatever contest is the contest of choice for teenage science geeks these days."

Rafe was nodding in agreement, but Charley could've said we'd start by lighting my physics text on fire and roasting marshmallows over it and he would've agreed. Now she checked my reaction. "Did I sound scary?"

"Absolutely," I said, not wanting to disappoint her.

"I'm totally getting the hang of this parenting thing."

"Sure," I said. "And studying isn't a bad idea. There's just one problem."

"What's that?" she asked.

13

"I don't think you understand what you're up against. Natalie called me a 'scientific black hole' today."

"But that's good, isn't it? It means you suck up information," said Charley.

"It means I suck up information and vaporize it. You could crack open my skull and there'd be nothing inside."

One of the things I like about Charley is that she can be stubborn and flexible at once. So instead of insisting on doing things her way, she asked, "What do you suggest, then? We can't just let you flunk."

"I suggest we concentrate on T.K., because she's the only person who can get me through the class and she's also the only person who can get me out of it. Not that she ever would, but maybe all of the foreign travel she's doing will broaden her perspective."

Charley thought this over. "Fair enough," she said. "As long as you pass your next quiz. And almost passing won't cut it. I can push Dr. Penske just so far before he blabs to Patty."

"I'll do my best," I said. "So long as you realize my best is seriously awful."

"Okay," she said. "It's a deal."

Rafe was as ready to agree to this new plan as he'd been to agree to anything else Charley said. He set his briefcase on the big table in the middle of the room and pulled out a roll of butcher paper. "I thought it would be useful to summarize the status of the investigation on a single page, but it

14

required a somewhat larger surface than a legal pad," he explained.

"You're like the Jack Kerouac of private eyes," said Charley. And then, when neither of us responded, *On the Road? A defining work of the Beat Generation? Typed on a continuous scroll more than one hundred and twenty feet long?"*

Rafe's scroll was only seven or eight feet long, and he unfurled it across the table as Charley and I anchored the corners with the salt and pepper shakers and a couple of bottles of hot sauce. He'd used a different colored marker for each aspect of the case, showing the potential connections with a rainbow's worth of arrows and interlocking circles.

Where most people would see chaos, Charley saw art. "Rafe, it's beautiful!" she said. "I didn't realize you had such a well-developed aesthetic sense."

This launched him on a fresh wave of blushing and stammering, so I left them to it and examined the list of suspects, written in bloodred ink at the center of the page.

At the top of the list were the members of EAROFO, a shady political action committee comprised of the chief executives of just about every major American oil company. EAROFO was an acronym for End American Reliance on Foreign Oil — which opening up an enormous new source of oil would definitely accomplish, whether it was legal or not.

A couple of months ago, T.K. heard a rumor through one of her environmental groups that EAROFO might be up to something questionable in Antarctica. She'd contacted the organization with what she'd thought was a generic request for information, but apparently it wasn't generic enough since we were pretty sure that's what raised the alarm on their end and set the plot against her in motion. We'd turned up evidence of our own pointing to EAROFO, too, but the clincher had been when the brown-haired woman I'd spotted leaving the offices of Navitaco, one of the EAROFO member companies, tried to lure me into the path of a speeding SUV.

So we were fairly confident EAROFO was behind everything — the group had the motive, means, and opportunity, which Rafe said were the three critical pieces of the puzzle. But we still didn't know who, specifically, within EAROFO was masterminding the operation, and given the power and resources of its members, figuring this out was going to be a challenge.

The list didn't end with EAROFO, either. We'd identified a couple of more secondary suspects as well. One was Thaddeus J. Wilcox IV, the chief operating officer of T.K.'s company, TrueTech. I'd always thought Thad was a weasel, and he'd done some strange things since my mother disappeared, like erasing the hard drive on her computer and trying to get Patience to sign papers giving him control of the company. Of course, Patience would never give up control of anything willingly, and she'd stymied him. But when I'd asked Thad point-blank if he was in on the whole conspiracy, he hadn't denied it — he'd only told me to "stop nosing around in other people's business" in a way that managed to be condescending and menacing at the same time.

So I wouldn't mind if we found out Thad was an evildoer. In fact, it would be fine by me. I felt a lot less fine, however, about our other suspect, since he was Quinn's dad, Hunter Riley. Hunter ran a hedge fund that traded energy stocks, and though he'd already made piles of money, he could make even bigger piles of money if he had advance knowledge about changes in the market for oil. He also had Trip Young, Navitaco's CEO, on his speed dial, which seemed excessive since Hunter's office was only a few floors above Trip's in a midtown skyscraper. They could've easily gotten together in person whenever they wanted to chat.

For obvious reasons, I was not so secretly hoping Hunter was innocent. After all, neutralizing Quinn's father wouldn't be the healthiest thing for our relationship. And with two kisses that definitely counted added to the one that possibly counted, I was starting to believe I could call it a relationship, which was a stunning thought all by itself.

Anyhow, we had our suspects, even if I did feel deeply conflicted about one of them. The catch was that we couldn't just organize a trip to Antarctica to get the evidence we needed, because it turned out that was a good way to get people interested in killing you. And going after any of the evildoers directly would be tough, especially if we didn't want them to know what we were trying to accomplish.

It took a while to come up with a plan, but we ultimately decided the best place to start was with the original crew from the *Polar Star*, to learn who had negotiated their replacement.

"I'll leave for Argentina tomorrow," Rafe said, rolling up the butcher paper and returning it to his briefcase. "Your mother will be able to tell me how she found the ship's captain initially, and I'll try to track him down." Rafe had a supersecret way to get in touch with T.K. — so secret he wouldn't even tell Charley and me, because he thought it was safest for us not to know. Which was frustrating, though he was probably right.

"And I'll see what I can learn from my sources, too," said Charley.

"What sources?" I asked.

"Oh, you know," she said mysteriously. "Sources."

"Fine," I said. "But what do I do while you're talking to your sources and Rafe's talking to his?"

Charley glanced at Rafe before answering. "Delia, you've got a lot going on already. Why don't you sit tight and let us take care of things for now?" Then, without pausing for breath, she changed the subject. "I don't know if you two are hungry, but I'm starving, and I'm thinking Wiener schnitzel and maybe spaetzle from that new Austrian place. They do make their waiters wear lederhosen, which seems cruel and possibly constitutes creating a hostile work environment, but maybe we can overlook that if the spaetzle's any good, because good spaetzle is hard to find, and perhaps you can't get good spaetzle without the

lederhosen, which would also explain why anyone wears lederhosen in the first place. What do you think?"

I thought sitting tight was the last thing I intended to do,
with or without spaetzle, and that Charley, of all people, should
know that.

But I just said, "Austrian sounds great."

Three

We ordered in Wiener schnitzel and spaetzle and also apple strudel, because Charley said one slice of strudel counted for at least two servings of fruits and vegetables. Then, when the delivery guy arrived and Charley decided he looked like Steve Sanders, Rafe made the mistake of asking if Steve Sanders was a friend of hers. Apparently he'd never watched the original *90210*, though it was syndicated in Colombia.

He had no idea what he was in for. Charley had the DVDs for all ten seasons, and she made us watch the pilot while we ate, providing commentary throughout. She even made Rafe promise he'd take the rest of the first season to watch on his flight to Argentina.

After dinner, as we were putting the dishes in the dishwasher, the phone rang — not Charley's cell or mine, but the landline in the loft. "Shall I?" offered Rafe, since Charley and I both had our hands full.

"No!" we yelled in unison. Besides telemarketers, only one person used that line, not that Charley had authorized her to do so — it was still a mystery how she'd obtained the unlisted number.

The answering machine picked up, and a moment later Patience's voice sliced through the room.

Charity, I know you're screening this call, and I find it inexcusable that a grown woman, however emotionally immature, is incapable of mustering the simple courtesy to speak to her own flesh and blood —

"As if there's anything but Ketel One flowing through her veins," said Charley.

— and instead cowers behind a mechanical device. What was Temperance thinking? The deplorable example you're setting for Cordelia —

"Deplorable," I agreed, and Charley shot me a look. I shrugged.

— I shudder to think. Now, Cordelia is expected for dinner on Thursday evening. Every child needs exposure to a wholesome family environment —

"Wholesome?" said Charley. "Has she ever met her kids?"

— and we have a responsibility to provide that for her. You are expected as well. Dinner will begin at half past seven, and

I expect you to arrive on time and in appropriate attire. As a reminder, appropriate does not — not! — include midriff-baring garments, garments that sparkle, overalls, or anything made of pleather. And don't bother to call with an excuse — I will not believe for a second time that you have a previous engagement with your macramé instructor.

Patience hung up with a brusque click, and Charley turned to me. "We certainly have our work cut out for us. It won't be easy to find midriff-baring sequined pleather overalls on such short notice. We might have to get them custom-made."

"I have ze perfect tailor!" announced a disembodied voice.

I shrieked, Charley jumped, and Rafe lunged for a weapon.

In a distant corner of the loft, an old sofa sat facing the windows. Now a head appeared above the sofa's back.

Charley let out a long, slow breath. "Dieter, what are you doing here?" she demanded.

"I vas attempting ze nap," Dieter answered, as if napping in other people's homes when they were completely unaware of your presence was the most natural thing in the world. "Zere is construction in my flat. But vith all ze talking and ze television, it is no better here. And zen, vith ze angry voman on ze phone, I give up."

"You know this man?" Rafe asked Charley, still brandishing the spatula he'd grabbed from the kitchen counter.

It's sort of hard to describe what, exactly, Charley does, since she's done so many things, but most recently she'd been starring in and coproducing Dieter's independent film. "Dieter's a director," Charley explained as she introduced him to Rafe. "His creative vision is absolutely revolutionary."

"I prefer *cineaste*," Dieter said. "Ze term director, it is so bourgeois." He was examining his reflection in the window, patting his spiky blond hair into just the right state of careful disarray and adjusting the drape of his scarf.

"And he has a key?" asked Rafe.

"But of course I have ze key," Dieter said.

"From when we were shooting up on the roof," Charley added, though she probably didn't even realize Rafe's initial alarm was rapidly giving way to jealousy.

Meanwhile, now that my pulse had returned to normal, I was worrying about what Dieter might have overheard. I'd thought only six people on this continent knew T.K. was alive: Charley, Rafe, Natalie, Quinn, the psychic I'd consulted, and me. But it looked like we might be up to seven. "Dieter, were you listening to everything this whole time?" I asked.

"Not everyzing," he said. "I vas dozing. But I zink you are vight to ask ze mother in Buenos Aires about ze ship captain. Zat is ze logical place to begin."

We had to ply him with leftovers, which led to a lengthy discussion of Austrian schnitzel versus German schnitzel and a dog he'd once had named Spaetzle, who had a penchant for Dadaist cinema, but Dieter ultimately seemed to recognize the importance of not sharing what he'd learned with anyone outside of the room. And though we didn't have any brilliant ideas about how best to deploy a cineaste, he was also eager to help.

"Zere must be a vay to harness ze power of visual media to furzer zis effort," he said, simultaneously stroking his goatee and furrowing his brow.

"We'll let you know if we think of anything," Charley told him. "But until then, not a word to anyone. And I still want my key back."

At school the next morning, it seemed like more people than usual were standing in little clumps out front before the bell rang, speaking in low, secretive voices, and then they were doing the same thing in the hallways between class periods and in the cafeteria.

"What's with everyone?" I asked Natalie at lunch.

"What do you mean?" she asked.

"Haven't you noticed the secretive whispering?"

Natalie's normally exceptionally perceptive, but now she looked around the cafeteria and then blankly back at me, like she didn't see anything out of the ordinary. "It's high school, Delia. What do you expect?"

She was totally oblivious, but she had a good excuse: A guy she'd met at one of those science fairs Charley had been threatening to send me to had texted her. She tried to pretend it wasn't a big deal, but as soon as I asked for the details it was like a dam broke. She couldn't stop gushing.

It was nice to hear Natalie obsessing about something other than what type of graduate degree she should pursue after college or which tech start-ups had the most family-friendly employment policies. For once she actually sounded like a regular, non-genius person. But after a half hour of gushing, my attention started to wander, and that's when I noticed the poster on a wall nearby: Prescott's annual Homecoming weekend was less than two weeks away.

West Palo Alto High had Homecoming, too, every fall. There'd be a football game against North Sunnyvale, with a tailgate party before and a dance in the courtyard after. I'd gone last year with friends, but it wasn't like I'd had a date. I'd never had a date of any sort back home.

But now I had Quinn, and that changed everything. Immediately, I started wondering if he'd ask me to the dance and, if so, what I should wear. I'd need to tell Charley — she'd want to make sure we found just the right outfit, and that meant shoes, too —

Natalie snapped her fingers in front of my face. "If you're thinking Quinn Riley is Homecoming King material, you are deeply, deeply confused," she said with a dismissive nod at the poster. "He's not exactly the school spirit type."

There was a segment of the student population Natalie had

labeled the Apathy Alliance, because they weren't interested in much of anything except, as she put it, "acting bored and spending their parents' money." She'd explained this on my first day at Prescott, citing Patience's kids, Gwyneth and Grey, as charter members. And I had to admit, in their case, it was pretty accurate. Personally, I called them the Ennui Twins, which was still a lot kinder than what Charley called them.

Of course, Natalie had also identified Quinn as the Alliance's de facto leader. And though Quinn did have a certain following among Alliance types — hence the minions — Natalie didn't know him the way I did. She'd never seen him rehearsing *Romeo and Juliet* or teaching his little brother and sister how to surf. Besides, anybody who kissed the way Quinn kissed me couldn't be apathetic. He might even be into the whole Homecoming thing.

Anyhow, Natalie eventually agreed to disagree on that topic so she could get back to gushing. Then the bell rang, and I spent the next two class periods trying to figure out an incredibly subtle way to bring up Homecoming when I saw Quinn in drama. But once class arrived, I was thwarted by Mr. Dudley, our drama teacher.

Usually Mr. Dudley waits until the final latecomer has straggled into the auditorium before he begins class. He perches on the edge of the stage with his leather portfolio open before him, pretending to be thinking deep, artistic thoughts or studying a script, but everyone knows he's really either texting his agent or admiring his latest headshots. He does happen to be unbelievably good-looking, but he also talks a lot about "channeling the Muse" with a phony British accent.

Today, however, he started class in a crazily punctual manner. We were due for new assignments, and I'd been hoping he'd pair me with Quinn again in more *Romeo and Juliet*. Instead he callously handed me Lady Macbeth's sleepwalking rant, the one where she's having nightmares about not being able to get the blood off her hands. He assigned monologues to the other juniors in the class, too.

So that was already sort of odd, though it's not like Mr. Dudley's mind functions in the most predictable way. But then, after essentially sentencing the juniors to solitary confinement, he cast all of the seniors, including Quinn and Gwyneth (who only takes drama because she's in love with Mr. Dudley and not because she's particularly interested in self-expression), in a scene from *The Crucible*.

They spent the entire period reading lines in a big group on the stage while the rest of us had to rehearse on our own in different parts of the auditorium. I ended up sitting alone in the last row of seats, mumbling "out, damned spot" to myself for the better part of an hour.

And then I was thwarted again, because Quinn was in a huge rush after class. There was barely time to say hi, much less delicately steer the conversation toward approaching school events.

"Sorry, I've got to run," he said, shoving the photocopied pages of his *Crucible* scene into his backpack. "I have that family thing, remember?"

I'd completely forgotten but now I asked, "What kind of family thing?"

"My dad's leaving tomorrow on a business trip so he and Fiona are insisting on quality time," he said as I followed him out of the auditorium. "We're going to an old James Bond movie at the Ziegfeld and then Bea and Oliver somehow got them to agree to Chuck E. Cheese for dinner. Kids under twelve get free refills on soda — we're going to have to pry them off the ceiling."

Fiona is Quinn's stepmother, and Bea and Oliver are his half siblings. As small kids go, they're pretty cute, but I was less concerned about their sugar and caffeine intake than I was about the alarm bells that had started blaring in my head when Quinn said Hunter was leaving town. "Where's your dad going?" I asked, trying my best to act like this was a normal sort of question.

"Who knows?" he said, holding the heavy door at the main entrance open for me. "I think it was somewhere that begins with an *A*. Argentina maybe? Hunter travels so much I never really pay attention anymore. It could be Abu Dhabi. Hey — I'd better hurry. I'll try to give you a call later."

And then he was off, without a kiss but just a shoulder squeeze to me and a passing hello to Charley, who was outside on the steps, waiting to escort me home.

"Everything okay?" asked Charley. I must have looked a bit disconcerted. After all, one of our suspects was potentially on his way to South America, and it didn't help that it was the suspect I'd been hoping was on our list entirely by mistake.

"Sure," I said, trying to sound convincing, but mostly I was doing some quick rationalizing in my head.

If Hunter was going to Argentina, I'd have to tell Charley, and Rafe, too, so he could warn T.K. But first I needed to confirm that Argentina really was Hunter's destination. I mean, there was no reason to get everyone all worked up if it turned out he was actually going to Albania or Algeria or some other A-named place.

At least, that's what I told myself, and it felt like it made sense at the time.

"Well, I have a fabulous idea for an after-school activity," said Charley. Charley has a lot of ideas, and she almost always thinks they're fabulous. "You, my dear niece, are tragically lacking in accessories, and I have been tragically remiss in not doing something about it sooner. I'm thinking Barney's as a warm-up, then there are a bunch of little boutiques in Nolita we should check out, and after Nolita we can hit a couple of those stands on Canal Street before finishing with dim sum in Chinatown. And then we have nine more seasons of *90210* waiting for us at home. How does that sound?"

It wasn't like I'd be able to talk to Quinn about Hunter's exact destination until later. If all went well, by the time we got back to the loft Quinn would be home from Chuck E. Cheese and could tell me Hunter was actually going to Alsace-Lorraine and Charley would be on such a post-shopping high she wouldn't even notice if her *90210* boxed sets went quietly missing. "That sounds perfect," I said.

"Then there's not a second to spare," said Charley. "We only have three hours and twenty-four minutes before stores start closing on us." She began hustling me down the steps.

At which point we almost crashed into Patience.

Four

Patience's normal walking pace was like a track star's idea of a sprint, but today she was moving so quickly her crisp Armani suit was a pin-striped blur, and the click-clack of her Blahniks on the stone steps sounded like machine-gun fire. Regardless, every blond highlight remained obediently in place.

"Ack!" cried Charley, leaping out of the way. I darted behind Charley — if I was lucky, Patience wouldn't even see me there.

But Patience didn't break stride. In fact, she didn't seem to notice us at all as she raced past and into the building.

Charley looked at me and I looked at her. "Okay," she said. "Even for Patty, that was bizarre."

I had to agree. I mean, it wasn't like Patience was the warmest and fuzziest person. If anything, she was pretty high on the cold and bristly list. And moments like this reminded me all over again that there must be some incredibly freakish mutations at work in the Truesdale DNA — that was the only way to reconcile T.K., Patience, and Charley showing up on the same branch of the family tree.

But Patience not stopping for three seconds to lower her Chanel sunglasses, icily acknowledge our presence, and say something about how Charley's batik silk jumpsuit and Sergio Rossi platform boots would be utterly inappropriate in any remotely civilized venue, much less on the Prescott campus?

Definitely bizarre.

"Come on," said Charley. "Let's get out of here while the getting's good." She hurried me into a conveniently passing taxi. "Barney's," she told the driver. "And step on it. Please. If you don't mind. Thank you."

He pulled away from the curb with a satisfying screech of tires, but Charley sighed anyway. "Saying 'please' and 'thank you' is the right thing to do, but it does ruin the overall effect."

"Do you think Dr. Penske got to Patience?" I asked as the cab sped down Fifth Avenue. "Was that why she was there?" My threat level, already elevated, had cranked up to Code Red. Though, now that I thought about it, Patience couldn't be meeting with Dr. Penske, since I'd seen him leave when Quinn had. Unless she intended to stake out his office until he returned tomorrow morning, but that seemed unlikely. People fit themselves around Patience's schedule, not the other way around.

"I called Dr. Penske this morning, to tell him we'd spoken about your quiz, and he promised he wouldn't say anything to Patty," said Charley. "He even said scout's honor, which actually means something when he says it, because did you know Dr. Penske is a den leader for his son's Cub Scout troop?"

I did know, because he mentioned it frequently in class, and whenever he did, Natalie would write me a frenzied note about how a man of science should be more aware of the scouting movement's fascist overtones and she'd enlighten him herself but was concerned doing so would negatively impact the recommendations she'd need Dr. Penske to write for her college applications (which, by the way, weren't due for another year and three months).

But I wanted to keep Charley focused, so I just said, "Then what was Patience doing there? She looked really —"

"Terrifying. I know."

"I was thinking more like determined. She's always terrifying."

"Well, she's always determined, too. What's even more bizarre is I left a message for her today and she never called back," said Charley.

"Why would you do that?" Patience had made it clear there was no need to RSVP for Thursday, not that Charley wasn't already planning on coming down with a severe communicable disease that would last precisely as long as dinner.

"I wanted to know whether she'd been in touch with Thad after she foiled his attempt to alienate you from the fruits of your mother's labor. I'd thought Patty would jump at the opportunity to make his life a living hell, not to mention that asking her to call me is an open invitation to make my life a living hell, or at least inviting a lecture on whatever I've done most recently to embarrass her, like breathing, and I thought she'd jump at that opportunity, too. But she hasn't made a peep in my direction all day. She's been completely peepless."

And somehow, silence from Patience was even more ominous than the alternative.

Charley's career path probably shouldn't be called a path, since it's been more a series of nonlinear hops from one unrelated activity to another. Before Dieter's film, she'd done stints in the Peace Corps, zoology, and Eastern medicine, though not necessarily in that order.

Somewhere along the way, she accidentally made some money, and thanks to our ancestor, Reginald Phineas Baxter Truesdale, who was an evil coal baron back in the nineteenth century, she inherited a lot, too. Having such a healthy bank account makes her feel guilty, so she gives money away to just about anyone who asks. She also likes to act as a one-woman retail stimulus package whenever time allows.

Barney's wasn't really Charley's style, nor, according to her, was it mine. But she still knew without checking the directory exactly where we wanted to be, which was in the accessories section of the Co-Op department on the seventh floor, and once we arrived she made Patience look like she was in training for the Slowpoke Olympics.

It took less than thirty seconds for her to pick out a Subversive choker with a bunch of gold chains and different lockets, though agonizing over a Dannijo cuff bracelet with a pattern of overlapping leaves and an Alkemie one with an elephant took several minutes at least. We ultimately agreed to buy both and share, though I suspected Charley's secret plan involved wearing them together.

I thought I'd be fully accessorized after that, but we took the subway down to Nolita, where we stopped to pick up several pairs of Erickson Beamon gypsy earrings before hitting a stand on Canal Street so Charley could get us matching I ❤ NY children's T-shirts. (Hers had gone missing in the wash and I'd never had one.) She capped it all off by buying an insane number of bangles from another stand for twenty bucks. She swore I'd find them indispensable, but she also believed the lady at the stand who said the bangles were real gold, so I wasn't sure what to think.

We wound up in Chinatown, at a crowded dim sum restaurant where everyone but us was speaking Cantonese. A continuous stream of passing waiters handed out little plates of dumplings and spring rolls from trolleys, tallying your bill based on the number of empty plates on your table when you finished.

Anyhow, as we were eating, Charley eventually got around to telling me about how she'd had coffee earlier with one of her mysterious sources, a man she'd met back when she'd decided to open an art gallery. This had been a short-lived venture, because while she liked being surrounded by art and hanging out with artists, the only people who'd been buying art at the time were Wall Street types.

"Let's just say that Patty would have wanted to invite all of these guys over for scotch and cigars. But after the market crashed, a lot of them lost their jobs and decided that meant they should get in touch with their own creative sides, because what the world has been lacking is the found-object sculpture of arbitrageurs."

"So you had coffee with somebody?" I prompted. Charley almost always does get to the point — sometimes she just needs an extra push to get her there.

"Brad," she said, accepting another plate of pot stickers from a passing trolley and setting it on the table between us. "A disproportionate number of these guys are named Brad, and I can guarantee you they also spent both their teen years and their twenties wearing their baseball caps backward, which is not a good look. This particular Brad is trying to be a stand-up comic, because he thinks it draws on the same set of skills he honed as a commodities trader."

I perked up. "Commodities like oil?" I asked.

"You are very clever, in addition to being well-accessorized," said Charley with visible pride.

"Thank you."

"You're welcome. So, yes, Brad traded oil futures. He still does, actually, but now he trades them in his pajamas at his kitchen table instead of in a Zegna suit at Lehman Brothers."

"And?"

"And he told me a couple of interesting things. First, the energy markets have been unusually volatile of late — prices are all over the place."

"What does that mean for us?" I asked.

"Well, Brad thinks the volatility is because there are even more rumors than usual floating around."

"What kind of rumors?"

And that's when the conversation ground to a halt. At least, Charley paused for a full three seconds before answering, which is like a regular person's conversation grinding to a halt.

She put down her chopsticks, leaving a pot sticker only half-eaten — a clear indication she was about to tell me something very serious — and I realized she'd been working up to whatever she was going to say next for a while.

Charley chose her words with care. "The rumors are that a very influential person has been making bets that the price of oil is going to head down. Seriously enormous bets. And way, way down."

"Oh?" I said, but my mind was already skipping ahead.

You didn't have to be a commodities trader to understand that whoever was making the bets must think there would be a lot more oil available soon, which would drive down prices. Which suggested this person knew what was going on in Antarctica, because it wasn't like there was an endless supply of as-yet-untapped sources of oil on the planet, particularly ones that were being secretly tapped. Which then suggested this person might also have been involved in trying to have T.K. killed, since she'd been planning on letting the world know what was happening, which would've made the bets he was placing worthless.

And all of this meant we should definitely be targeting this person in our investigation.

But based on the way Charley was acting, it was pretty obvious we already were.

Five

Meanwhile, Charley was still talking. "You know I hate to be the bearer of bad news, and I hope you remember you're not supposed to kill or shoot or otherwise punish the messenger, especially when the messenger has just bought you a fabulous selection of accessories she fully intends to borrow only on those rare occasions when she has your explicit permission to do so, but the influential person who's betting the price of oil is going down —"

I finished her sentence for her. "Is Hunter Riley."

She seemed relieved that I was the one who actually said his name. "Sadly, yes. And I don't see why he'd be making those bets unless he really is in on the whole thing."

I might have been able to convince myself temporarily that Quinn hadn't remembered correctly where Hunter was heading the next day. But combined with what Charley had learned, it was all sort of incriminating. And now I had no way to rationalize not telling Charley, even before I could ask Quinn about Hunter's exact destination.

She was a bit upset I hadn't told her right away, but since it had taken her almost as long to work up the courage to share the details of her conversation with Brad, she could hardly hold my rationalizing against me. Instead she insisted I eat the remaining pot sticker as she settled the check and gathered our shopping bags. Then, as soon as we hit the street, she texted Rafe. He'd be picking up his messages when he landed in Buenos Aires.

Rafe had cautioned us against discussing the investigation over the phone — if the bad guys were powerful enough to get away with illegally tapping into Antarctic oil fields, they could probably arrange to listen in on our calls or read our messages without too much trouble. But that meant we needed a way to communicate when we weren't safely inside the loft or surrounded by non-English speakers, so we'd worked out a code.

Of course, this actually meant Charley had worked out a code, since Rafe seemed to lose any capacity for independent thought in her presence and I'd already learned that sometimes it was easiest just to let her have her way. And though she could have used *A*, *B*, and *C* or something like that to reference our various suspects, such a straightforward solution would never have occurred to her.

As a result, our suspects were now code-named after the Chipmunks. EAROFO was Alvin, since we thought whoever was orchestrating everything there was the principal trouble-maker. Thad was Simon, because he was so nerdy, and Hunter was Theodore, because we'd still been hoping he'd turn out to be harmless. And in case that wasn't convoluted enough, Argentina was Madonna, because Madonna had starred in a movie about Eva Perón, who'd been the first lady of Argentina, and Charley had been a Madonna fan since her very first album.

Anyhow, this is what Charley ended up texting Rafe:

Theo visiting Madonna — confirmation pending

I wasn't altogether confident Rafe would remember Theodore was supposed to be Hunter — he knew less about the Chipmunks than he knew about teen prime-time soaps — but he should get the Madonna part since Charley had found a clip of Madonna in *Evita* on YouTube and played it for us twice. That should be sufficient for him to put T.K. on preliminary alert.

Which brought us to our next problem. Because before I could even get in touch with Quinn for the confirmation, Charley felt obligated to give me a minilecture on how while Quinn might be a stand-up guy, we now had more reason than ever to believe his father wasn't, which implied I needed to be extra careful when it came to what I told him.

To be clear, it wasn't like Quinn didn't already know T.K. was still alive. After all, he was the one who'd loaned me the money to hire Rafe in the first place. He'd also been there with me the previous week, when Rafe showed up with the picture of T.K. he'd taken less than thirty-six hours earlier, somewhere on the outskirts of Santiago. In fact, our second kiss occurred that same afternoon, and since it hadn't been in the context of *Romeo and Juliet*, it was the first one that definitely counted.

After that, though, Charley and Rafe made me swear not to tell Quinn anything more about the investigation. This had turned out to be easier than I'd thought it would be, since we hadn't had much private time. Quinn spent the weekend at his family's place in Southampton, and this week there'd only been the quick snatches of conversation after school. It was just like Quinn had said — we were logistically star-crossed.

But now I was beginning to wonder if it was more than logistics. Because on the walk back to the loft, as I was explaining all of the logistical problems to Charley, I realized something startling:

Quinn hadn't been asking me for the details on the investigation, not even on those few occasions when we'd been alone together. Last week he'd wanted to know everything, but after that it was like he'd forgotten any of it ever happened.

And that was strange. In fact, it was downright disturbing, particularly when I took into account the way today's kiss good-bye hadn't been a kiss but a wholly unsatisfying shoulder squeeze. Sure, there'd been a lot of people around, including my aunt, but still — a shoulder squeeze?

I froze in place, right there on the sidewalk. "Oh, no."

"Oh, no what?" asked Charley, stopping alongside me. We were both oblivious to the resulting pedestrian pileup behind us.

"Quinn hasn't asked about the investigation."

She shrugged. "Maybe he understands you shouldn't be talking about it, and he doesn't want to put you in an awkward position. Or maybe he has other things on his mind."

"Maybe he doesn't have other things on his mind. Maybe he's losing interest."

"Excuse me?" said Charley.

"What if Natalie's right about Quinn's essential nature? What if the last couple of weeks were an aberration, and now he's reverting to his normal apathetic state, where first he stops caring about the investigation and then he stops caring about me? It's like in that book with the lab rat, only instead of intelligence it's emotion, and he's already peaked."

"Are you insane?" said Charley. She took me by the arm and began steering me briskly along the sidewalk, like she was a nurse and I was a patient who'd wandered away from the psych ward. "First, if you're talking about *Flowers for Algernon*, it was a mouse, not a rat. And second, please, please tell me you're not turning into one of those girls."

"One of which girls?"

"One of those awful girls who spends all her time obsessing about some guy and dissecting his every single word and action for hidden meaning because if he's tied his shoes with a double knot that means true love but a single knot means he's moved on. I'll tell you now: Quinn is totally into you. It's absolutely, blindingly clear to anybody who's seen you together. And when we get

43

home, you're going to call him and once you've finished finding out for sure whether or not his father's off to Argentina, you'll end up cooing at each other like little lovebirds and all will be well."

Even under the best of circumstances I would've had doubts about the cooing lovebirds part, but I recognized Charley had a lot more experience in romantic matters than I did, which wasn't hard since I had none. And I did need to confirm Hunter's destination, too. So as soon as I thought there was a reasonable chance Quinn's family outing had ended, I called him. And I had to admit, he sounded perfectly fine.

I mean, it wasn't like he confessed his undying love or anything, but the conversation felt easy, the way it usually feels once I get past the brain paralysis. He wasn't cool or aloof or indifferent. And I even managed to work in the Argentina question in a way that actually seemed to fit, though I didn't get a chance to bring up Homecoming.

"How was Chuck E. Cheese?" I asked.

"The kids drank a gallon of Coke each, so they won't get to sleep until sometime next year, but we all made it through in one piece. Or as close to one piece as Bea and Oliver will ever be." I could hear them chattering in the background, along with assorted clattering and clanking. "They also won a bunch of prizes that require assembly, so now my dad's trying to put everything together, and he's not the handiest guy. He's probably looking forward to eleven hours alone on a plane."

44

Eleven hours was about the length of Rafe's flight from New York to Buenos Aires. "It's Argentina, then?" I asked as casually as I could. Charley was not so secretly listening in on my side of the conversation, and she silently applauded my subtlety from across the room.

"Yeah. And do you want to hear something scary?"

"Sure."

Quinn lowered his voice. "I know I don't always pay attention when Hunter says where he's going, but when I do pay attention, at least I have some general idea what he's talking about. But I don't think Fiona gets the difference between Mexico and Argentina. She kept making Hunter promise he'd bring back piñatas for the kids. And that's when she wasn't warning him to go easy on the margaritas and reminding him nachos are high in saturated fat —"

There was a sudden crash behind him, followed by several thumps, and either Bea or Oliver or possibly both began to shriek, so loudly I automatically held the phone away from my ear so I wouldn't burst an eardrum.

And by the time I got the phone back to my ear, I'd missed most of whatever Quinn said after that. All I caught was "emergency room" and "'night, Juliet."

Then he was gone, before I could even say good night back.

Six

The next morning, I tried to convince Charley I was perfectly capable of getting around town without an escort. After all, nobody had tried to kill me in nearly a week — it was entirely possible the evildoers had decided they shouldn't be worried about a sixteen-year-old Prescott student or, even better, forgotten about me altogether. But Charley still insisted on taking me to school, though she refused to talk about Quinn.

"I might be done having that discussion," she announced on the walk to the subway. "A million times in twelve hours is a lot, especially when we were only awake for four of those hours."

"It hasn't been anywhere near a million times," I said.

"It certainly seems that way, at least it does from the perspective of a sane and rational person," said Charley, apparently unaware that sane and rational people tend not to wear outfits made entirely of purple corduroy, complete with a matching rhinestone-studded beret. "However, because I am your kindest and most understanding aunt, not that Patty offers much competition, I'll say this one final time: Quinn likes you. He was also concerned his siblings might be in mortal danger,

46

and I think that's a legitimate reason for him to get off the phone without causing you to question his affections. It wasn't like he suddenly decided he had to take up quilting or feed his pet sea monkeys."

"But —"

"Delia, I recognize developing confidence in a new relationship can be challenging, but you are the star of your own movie, not a supporting actress in Quinn's movie. You don't merely react to others; you determine how your own plot unfolds."

Sometimes I wondered if Charley even made sense to herself. "But —"

"Not discussing it," she said.

"But —"

Charley stuck her fingers in her ears and started singing "Holiday" out loud — ever since the code-drafting session, she'd had Madonna's greatest hits playing nonstop in the loft — and she kept singing for the rest of the walk to the subway, which was still several blocks away. She only stopped after we'd descended into the station and she needed her fingers to get her MetroCard from her wallet.

"I have a brilliant idea," she said as we waited on the platform for an uptown train. "Why don't you try obsessing about Quinn with somebody else? Like Natalie. Or one of your friends from Palo Alto. Or anyone at all whose tremendous, saintlike patience hasn't been worn dangerously thin by having to repeat the same advice over and over and over again."

Charley had a point, though I didn't think I could handle Natalie's tough love on this topic. It was possible she'd be more indulgent now that she had a crush of her own, but indulgent for Natalie might still leave a lot of people emotionally scarred. On the other hand, talking to Erin, my best friend from home, wasn't such a bad —

My heart did that sinking thing it does when you realize you might have done something unforgivable. I tore open the clasp on my book bag and began frantically searching for my phone.

"What's the date?" I asked Charley.

"September," she said. "Or maybe October? It could be October. I do know it's a Wednesday. It is Wednesday, right?"

I located my phone at the very bottom of the bag and dug it out, hoping it would tell me it wasn't too late. But when I saw the date on the screen, my heart sank even further.

I'd missed Erin's birthday.

And not just by one day, either. She'd turned seventeen a full forty-eight hours ago, and for the first time since we'd met at Palo Alto Montessori, I hadn't been there to celebrate with her. Which would've been okay if I'd bothered to send a gift or call or make any effort whatsoever to show her I actually cared. Instead I'd completely spaced.

The worst part was that she probably wasn't even angry. Knowing Erin, she'd made excuses for me, telling herself I hadn't forgotten because I was a negligent friend but only because I had other things to worry about, what with being recently orphaned and miserable in a cold, unfeeling city three thousand miles away.

Which just made me feel all the more negligent, since it was so far from the truth. I mean, I wasn't orphaned, not really, and while I was definitely looking forward to having T.K. back for good, Rafe had assured me she'd be safe as long as she took the proper precautions. And T.K. was like a poster child for proper precautions — we had a fully stocked first aid kit in every single room of the house in California, not to mention both the glove compartment and the trunk of the Prius, and neither of us was particularly accident-prone.

And as for being miserable in a cold, unfeeling city — well, that wasn't exactly accurate, either. I'd be wearing my I ❤ NY T-shirt at that very moment if I didn't have to wear a uniform to school. Somehow, it was all both new and right at the same time, even when I was worrying about Quinn's emotions potentially seeping away in a slow but irreversible decline.

The fact of the matter was there was only one real problem with the entire situation, and that was it was beginning to feel normal. Like this was home, and Palo Alto was a nice place where I'd lived a long time ago, back in some other life.

Which might complicate things when T.K. did return.

A brightening gleam of light from the mouth of the tunnel signaled the train's approach, and thirty seconds later it pulled into the station with a screeching wail of brakes. The doors slid open, and we squeezed ourselves in with the other rush-hour passengers. Then the doors slid shut, the train left the station, and people started staring at us.

There might have been some strange glances before, out on the sidewalk, but I'd chalked that up to Charley's singing. And for the first couple of stops, we were busy talking about how I could make up for missing Erin's birthday, so I didn't catch on right away. But once I did notice, it was impossible to ignore, and it just got more and more creepy at each stop, as some of the people who'd been staring would get off and new people would get on, take their places, and start staring at us, too.

When I saw a woman nudge another woman and point at us, like we were chimpanzees at the zoo, I couldn't take it anymore. Charley was telling me about a service that would send Erin an ice sculpture carved from our own original design, but she stopped talking when I elbowed her. I had to stand on tiptoe to whisper in her ear. "People are staring at us," I said.

"I know," she whispered back. "I was hoping you hadn't noticed."

"How could I not notice? What do you think is going on?"

"I have no clue —" she started to say.

And then we pulled into the station at 51st Street, the doors opened, and suddenly, everything became clear.

Charley gave a yelp. "I don't believe it," she said in shock.

I was speechless, so I couldn't reply.

"I'm going to kill him," said Charley as the doors shut. "Kill him."

Through the windows the tiled wall of the station began to blur as the train picked up speed, but I could still see the row of billboards, with the same image on each: the moment Charley and I first met.

It was from the night Dieter had been filming up on the roof of her building, when I'd accidentally wandered onto the set. Charley stood with her hands on her hips, looking imposing and glamorous in a red satin dress. I was also standing with my hands on my hips but looked far less imposing and glamorous since I was wearing jeans.

"What does Dieter think this is going to accomplish?" demanded Charley, as if I'd have any idea. "Is this what he meant by harnessing the power of visual media?"

I was still speechless, so I still didn't reply.

"I'm going to kill him," Charley said again.

There wasn't any text on the billboards — just the two of us, standing there for no obvious reason. And judging by the way people had been staring before we reached 51st Street, there were similar billboards at other subway stations.

"Yes," said Charley, not in response to anything I'd said but as if she'd definitively resolved an internal debate. "Dieter must die. I'm not going to tell you how, because that might make you an accomplice, but rest assured it will be a slow and painful experience for him."

Charley had her phone out and Dieter's number pulled up before we'd reached the station for Prescott, and she pressed SEND as soon as she had reception. Not surprisingly, his number went straight to voice mail. If Dieter had even half a brain, he'd hightail it out of the country before Charley could strangle him with his own scarf, and he'd stay away until she had an opportunity to calm down.

I couldn't say I was thrilled, either, though I took some comfort in the knowledge that I didn't have to worry about what people would say at school — hardly anybody at Prescott would have seen the billboards, since doing so involved public transportation. Except for the faculty and a few kids on financial aid, the Prescott community traveled by limo, car service, or taxi.

I only hoped the evildoers were equally subway-averse.

Seven

Rage made Charley walk faster, which also might explain why Patience was always so speedy. We arrived at Prescott a full ten minutes before the first bell.

Even though we were early, there were so many people out front it looked like school had already started but the building had been evacuated. Practically the entire student body and half the faculty had collected on the broad steps leading up to the main entrance, and they were all standing around in groups of two and three and four, talking intently in low voices.

"Is something special happening today?" asked Charley, taking in the mass of people.

"Not that I know of," I said. It was possible there'd been an announcement of some sort, but I hadn't been doing such a great job of paying attention lately.

Then a silver van pulled up and double-parked on the street, fencing in the headmaster's Volvo in its reserved spot at the curb. This was like the Prescott equivalent of aggravated assault and treason combined, so a hush fell over the crowd, but the murmur of voices resumed with even greater intensity when two guys got out of the van. They wore matching black suits and white shirts, and each carried an aluminum attaché case. Wordlessly, they marched up the steps and disappeared inside.

"Was that the Secret Service?" asked Charley. "Is the president coming?"

I might not have been as attentive as I should be, but I was pretty sure I'd remember if the president was visiting Prescott. "They weren't talking into their wrists, and they didn't have the wire thingies coming out of their collars," I said.

"Or the mirrored glasses," Charley agreed, but she was disappointed. "I've always wanted to go out with a Secret Service agent, and they're so hard to meet. This would have been a perfect opportunity."

"Now I know what you're looking for, I'll keep my eyes peeled."

"That's sweet of you. Though eye peeling sounds disgusting so maybe you shouldn't."

"I don't think I'll be running into many Secret Service agents anyway," I said.

"It's probably better that you don't. But if it's not the president and that wasn't the Secret Service, and since I don't see any SWAT teams or bomb squads, I'm going to assume it's nothing to worry about and track down Dieter. Unless you want me to stay until we know what's going on, because I can if you want me to . . ."

Her voice petered out. We'd both spotted Gwyneth across the street, and she was heading in our direction.

"I'll be fine," I told Charley.

"It's not that I'm a complete coward," she said. "I'm brave about a lot of things — I love the dentist, and snakes, too — but Patty's kids strike fear in my heart. I always worry whatever they have is catching."

"Really, it's okay," I said. "Save yourself."

Charley flashed a grateful smile and disappeared in a streak of purple corduroy. Gwyneth was a lot more snail-like — it was part of the ennui thing — so I had several long moments to steel myself before she meandered up.

"Hey," she said, stifling a yawn. Her lip gloss and icy blue eyes were the only color in her pale face, and her white-blond hair hung listlessly down her back.

"Hey," I said back, and waited for her either to stroll past or say whatever she was there to say. Usually she only spoke to me when Patience told her to.

"How are you?" she said.

"Uh, I'm fine, thanks. How are you?"

"Fine," she said, like small talk was normal for us.

And then she just stood there, next to me, like it was also perfectly normal for us to hang out together instead of with our respective friends, or, in my case, Natalie. Though, now that I looked around, I realized I didn't see any of Gwyneth's friends. I didn't even see Grey anywhere. In fact, a lot of the seniors seemed to be missing, including Quinn and his various minions.

"Crazy, isn't it?" said Gwyneth.

I assumed this was in reference to the crowd and not to the fact she was still standing next to me or to the way she could speak without moving her lips. "I don't know if it's crazy or not, because I have no idea what's going on," I admitted.

"You didn't hear?" she said.

"Hear what?" I asked.

"You don't know?"

"I don't know."

"You really don't know?"

"No, I really don't know."

"How do you not know?"

"I don't know how I don't know, but I'd like to know." I managed to say this politely, but the conversation was getting a bit frustrating.

"They're probably going to get kicked out," she said.

"Wait — who's getting kicked out?"

"All of them."

"All of who? Or whom?"

"Everyone involved."

"Involved in what?"

"The poker thing," she said.

To her credit, she didn't actually say "obviously" — she just implied it. And though it took a while to get it out of her, she ultimately did tell me the whole story, and she was right: It was crazy.

It turned out that a bunch of seniors, including Grey and several other Alliance members, had started up their own online business. And when Gwyneth first told me this, I didn't understand what the problem was. If anything, it showed a level of initiative that seemed like a healthy departure from their usual lack of productive activity. So this shouldn't have been a big deal.

Except for the part where their business was targeting under-age poker players, and the other part where they'd been operating the whole thing from the Prescott campus.

Apparently there was an old server the school no longer used, and it had been gathering dust in the computer center's storage closet. I didn't want to know what Grey and his friends had been doing in the closet, but they found the server and decided it would be perfect for hosting a gambling site. And in another genius move, they neglected to arrange for their own Internet connection and piggybacked on Prescott's broadband network instead.

The insane thing was that they might have gotten away with it if they'd been less successful. But within a few hours of launching, the site was generating hundreds of hits, and by the second day they had thousands of kids logged in and playing poker around the clock, using their parents' credit cards to place their bets. And the more people played poker, the more bandwidth the site sucked up, and that's what did them in.

The site went live on Friday, and by Monday, Prescott's

Internet service provider was calling, because the huge amount of bandwidth being used on campus was compromising service to everyone else in the neighborhood. By Tuesday morning, the administration had located the server, still in the storage closet but plugged in and humming with so much activity it was practically smoking, and by Tuesday afternoon, they'd started identifying the students involved and alerting their parents.

As school scandals went, this was pretty major — it definitely accounted for the whispering the previous day. It also explained Patience's bizarre behavior. She hadn't been on her way to see Dr. Penske — she'd been on her way to see Mr. Seton, the headmaster, to try to prevent Grey from being expelled.

And the scandal was still unfolding. Mr. Seton was determined to root out anybody who'd had even the slightest involvement.

"It's like a total witch hunt," Gwyneth told me. "Seton interrogated me for an hour yesterday, but Grey and I haven't been speaking since he stepped on my Tom Ford sunglasses, so I was completely out of the loop."

Meanwhile, the two guys in the black suits were from a computer security firm. The site had already been shut down, but they were supposed to be analyzing the network traffic and data logs and all of the other digital evidence to see if they could identify additional culprits.

The bell rang then, and we headed off to our separate classrooms. The whispering in the hallways continued between classes, but now that I knew what it was about, it didn't bother me. Only when Natalie and I got to lunch and were talking the whole thing over did I give it any more thought.

I had to admit, I never would've guessed Grey was capable of something like this. I could count the interactions I'd had with him on one hand, and I didn't need more than part of another hand to count the total number of words he'd said on all of those occasions put together. And while getting the poker site up and running might not require a lot of speech, it would definitely require more than staring idly into space.

But as Natalie pointed out, Grey was probably only a follower in this situation. "And it's not just Grey," she said. "The dubious legality of online gambling, particularly targeting the high school demographic, and the decision to use Prescott resources were substantial design flaws, but otherwise this was a well-conceptualized operation. The reason Headmaster Seton is still rounding people up is that nobody they've caught so far has the intellect and personal magnetism to pull this off."

"Who does?" I asked. "Have the intellect and personal magnetism, I mean."

"I can't say for sure, not without proof, but I have a theory," said Natalie.

"What's your theory?"

She gave me an odd look. "Can't you guess?"

"No," I said.

"You can't?"

"I can't."

"You're absolutely certain you can't?"

I felt like I was talking to Gwyneth again. "Absolutely certain."

"Think about the people who've already been caught. What do they all have in common?"

"I don't really know any of them, except Grey, and I wouldn't know him if we weren't related. And I have my doubts about that, but nobody will let me test his DNA."

"You don't need to know them well or be related to them — you just need to know there's only one person who's sharp enough to think this up and who they'd all follow off a cliff, and you must know who that is, because you'd follow that person off a cliff yourself."

I could hear Charley's voice in my ear, asking what following someone off a cliff actually meant — was it a real cliff, and if so, what was at the bottom, because if it was water or a stack of mattresses or a trampoline that was one thing, but if it wasn't, that would be something completely different — but I tried to concentrate. I couldn't imagine following anybody at Prescott anywhere, except Natalie, and, obviously, Qui —

I didn't consciously finish my thought, but the answer must have shown on my face anyhow.

"Exactly," said Natalie.

60

Eight

"Quinn wouldn't have," I said. "He couldn't have."

"Why not?" said Natalie.

I searched for a response. "He sucks at math."

"Why would he need math?" she asked. "It's not like he was writing the code or keeping the books — he could always delegate the menial tasks. No, what he needed was imagination and charisma, and you know Quinn has plenty of both."

I couldn't argue with that. Quinn was always doing things that weren't part of the program for a typical Upper East Side guy, like surfing and experimental theater, which definitely showed imagination. As for charisma, nobody else gave me brain paralysis just by walking into a room.

And that's when the realization hit me, like a wave of freezing water: The launch of the poker site coincided almost exactly with when Quinn had stopped asking about T.K.

It took a moment to process what that could mean, but once I did, I wished I hadn't. Because maybe Charley was right — Quinn wasn't being apathetic or losing interest — he'd had something else on his mind. And that something else was being the brains behind a gambling scheme that could get him expelled.

Which was disturbing all on its own, but it also led to the most disturbing thought yet: Simply put, if Quinn was the brains behind the operation, then he was actually a moron.

I mean, it would be one thing to find out he had an entrepreneurial streak. But he should have known better than to involve himself in something that might not be legal and to do it here at school to boot. It wasn't like he needed the money, either, and nobody had mentioned anything about how the proceeds were being used to shelter a homeless family or fund an arts program for underprivileged children.

And Quinn being moronic was a huge problem. Getting my head around that would throw everything I knew and thought and wanted into question.

Getting my heart around it might be impossible.

I put down my half-eaten grilled cheese and pushed the plate away. I'd lost my appetite.

I knew without asking how Charley would tell me to handle this situation, which was to ask Quinn directly instead of spinning imaginary scenarios and getting increasingly upset. So, gathering up what little courage I had, I spent the remainder of my lunch period trying to track him down.

But he was nowhere to be found. Not in the senior lounge, which I'd never set foot in before but was nearly empty today, and not on the stairwell landing where he sometimes hung out between classes. And then, last period, he wasn't even in drama.

It wasn't just Quinn, either. When I arrived in the auditorium, most of the seniors were missing, some because they'd been suspended pending further disciplinary action and others because they were sequestered in the library, waiting their turn to be called into Mr. Seton's office for interrogation. The ones who did make it to class were either confirmed loners who might be plotting other forms of mayhem but would never be associated with something as mainstream as gambling, or the type who'd trip over themselves to be the first to report anybody doing anything the slightest bit suspicious.

And, of course, Gwyneth, who seemed to think we were best friends now that her actual friends were unavailable. As Alliance members, they'd all been either implicated already or swept up in Mr. Seton's dragnet.

"Hey," she said, plopping herself down on the patch of stage right next to me. Even weirder, the corners of her lips angled the tiniest bit upward, almost like a smile.

Class, meanwhile, turned out to be a lecture from Mr. Dudley on parallels between *The Crucible* and "the machinations of a rigid establishment intent on crushing the creative spark," not that he mentioned Mr. Seton or anyone else by name. It was better than having to sit alone in a corner again doing Lady Macbeth, but it also made me wonder if Mr. Dudley was involved in the poker ring himself. He seemed to be taking the whole thing sort of personally.

Anyhow, he was so wrapped up in his speech — pacing and waving his arms around — that it was easy to reach into my bag and send Quinn a quick text, though it was a struggle to figure out what to say. I settled on the bare minimum:

Where r u? What's happening?

This seemed more diplomatic than asking him if he was, in fact, a moron and also more likely to preserve the potential for a relationship if it turned out he wasn't. Then I just sat there on the stage next to Gwyneth, pretending to listen to Mr. Dudley while in reality I waited for Quinn to text back and tried to shush the competing voices in my head.

It's not like I have a split personality, and I do have one continuous mental voice that's entirely mine, but a lot of the time it gets drowned out by the voices of other people that occasionally take up residence, all talking at once and buffeting my thoughts in different directions.

Charley was the loudest today, telling me I had nothing to worry about, but she might definitely be done discussing Quinn. Natalie came in second, making her neatly reasoned case against Quinn and lining up the evidence in an orderly row. Madonna was there, too, singing "Holiday," and Quinn himself put in a cameo. So all in all it was pretty noisy.

Then, suddenly, the noise stopped, and a single voice took over. It was my mother, and she was telling me to keep my eye on the ball.

This was a strange thing for her to say since she's not exactly the athletic type — the only sneakers she owns are white leather Tretorns she has polished at the shoe place whenever they get scuffed. She does like hiking, but that's more about communing with nature than exercise. Ash was my athletic parent, though he was never big on sports metaphors, either, maybe because he grew up in India, where they mostly play cricket, and maybe because he always preferred extreme sports like ice sailing and parkour to baseball or football or anything like that.

But it was still pretty obvious what T.K. meant. It was embarrassing, too, because in her no-nonsense way she was asking me to confront an ugly truth.

And the ugly truth was that I'd completely lost track of what I was supposed to be doing. It wasn't just that I didn't have my eye on the ball — I wasn't even on the field or at the stadium, or whatever the right sporty metaphor might be.

Because instead of focusing on the evildoers, I'd been obsessing over a guy, like one of those awful girls Charley had warned me about, and reacting to others rather than making the plot unfold myself. And while it probably wasn't realistic to expect I'd give up on obsessing over Quinn anytime soon, I couldn't deny my priorities had gotten totally messed up.

After all, it had been nearly forty-eight hours since Charley,

Rafe, and I had discussed the next phase of the investigation. I'd promised myself then I'd take action, even if Charley told me to sit tight and eat spaetzle.

But in the time that had elapsed I'd accomplished exactly nothing. If anything, I'd accomplished less than nothing, since I'd lost two days' worth of potential progress. I'd been too wrapped up in myself to pay attention to what was really important.

So, while Mr. Dudley lectured on, I resolved that now I would plunge into the investigation with laserlike focus. And I also realized who could point me in exactly the right direction — I'd reach out to her as soon as I possibly could.

Though given who it was, I shouldn't have been surprised when she reached out to me first.

Nine

I tried to lose Gwyneth after class, but it was like I'd accidentally adopted a stray puppy that didn't have any endearing puppy qualities.

Under normal circumstances I would've felt sorry for her — she wasn't used to being on her own. But today I needed to put Charley in an accommodating frame of mind, and that was much less likely to happen with Gwyneth around.

So when class was over, I gave Gwyneth my sunniest smile, hoping so much positive feeling would send her fleeing. And to make it clear I thought we were parting, I said, "Well, I'm off. See you tomorrow."

"Yeah," she said, like she understood.

Except then she followed me out of the auditorium and down the corridor. She even waited while I made an unnecessary stop at my locker in an attempt to shake her.

By the time we reached the steps out front, I'd resigned myself to her presence. In fact, I was thinking I might be able to use it to my advantage, because there was someone I wanted to see, and I couldn't let Charley know. But if I got rid of Charley by telling her I'd be hanging out with Gwyneth, she'd only worry

67

about me losing my mind and not that I might be up to anything she'd prefer me not to be up to.

Anyhow, I was so busy planning what I'd say to Charley that it took me a moment to notice she wasn't there. She'd sent a text instead.

> sorry sorry sorry — still hunting Dieter
> don't take subway alone — not safe
> ask Q 2 take u or put u in cab?
> $ in drawer/menus on counter/90210 next 2 TV
> sorry again

I returned my phone to my bag, marveling at how conveniently everything had worked out. Of course, I'd still have to get rid of Gwyneth before heading to the Lower East Side.

But when I looked up, I saw I wouldn't even need to make the trip: Carolina Cardenas was waving from the sidewalk.

"Why do you have the surprise? You are wanting to see me, *sí*?" said Carolina. Psychics tend to be a few steps ahead of other people, and sometimes Carolina forgot others lacked her special gifts. "Your auntie, she is not coming, so I will be your *músculo* today."

"What's a *músculo*?" I asked.

"Muscle," said Gwyneth, who I guessed took Spanish. For reasons I won't go into except to say they weren't mine, I'd always taken Latin, and that didn't help with Carolina. She was newly transplanted to New York from Ecuador, and her English could be spotty.

Carolina flexed her biceps, which, like the rest of her, were tiny. "Power yoga."

"Impressive," said Gwyneth. Then she turned to me. "Why do you need muscle?"

Just about everyone at school, including Gwyneth, thought the Range Rover incident had been random rather than part of a broader web of events. And Charley and I had also carefully kept Patience uninformed — she was convinced T.K. was dead and I was in denial, and she was still making noises about my being in need of psychiatric help — so I wasn't about to tell Gwyneth why I wasn't supposed to be going anywhere alone. "It's hard to explain," I said, which was true.

"Okay," said Gwyneth. And she wandered away.

Carolina yawned. "The cousin, I am looking in her head, and it makes me sleepy."

"I think it makes her sleepy, too," I said.

"You and I, we have no time for sleep," she said, motioning for me to follow her. "We have much to do."

Rafe on bodyguard duty was one thing — he did claim he knew karate, though I had a feeling he might be exaggerating about the black belt — but Carolina's psychic powers would be her only weapon if things turned violent. She was even shorter than I was, and while she liked to compensate by wearing five-inch heels, they just made her look like a little girl playing

69

dress-up. Her brown hair hung in loose waves down to her waist, and she seemed to do most of her shopping (except for the shoes, obviously) in the children's department at Target.

"Where are we going?" I asked.

"To your auntie's house," she said, teetering along in pink stilettos. "She will not be home until late, and her *televisión* is superior to my *televisión*. There is a program you must see."

"Which program?"

"*Bewitched*," she said. "Do you know it? Little Tabitha, she is my favorite."

I'd been expecting *Oprah* or maybe a *telenovela*, not that those would have made immediate sense, either. But back when everyone thought T.K. was dead, Carolina had known she was alive, and while she hadn't been able to pinpoint T.K.'s location on a map, her description exactly matched the part of Chile where she'd turned up. So now I'd do anything Carolina wanted, even if it meant watching a TV show that practically predated TV. "I've seen it a couple of times, I think."

"It is on all day. *Cómo se dice*, a marathon. And this morning, I see the advertisement, and you go pop in my head, and also the Sagittarius. I do not know why this is, but it is possible I will know better if we are viewing together."

A couple of weeks earlier, Carolina had called to warn me about a Sagittarius. Not that she could identify which specific Sagittarius posed the threat, but she was convinced one was out there and filled with evil intent.

We still hadn't gotten to the bottom of this, though when I'd told Natalie, who had issues with psychics, she'd helpfully pointed out that she herself was a Sagittarius, as were one-twelfth of the other seven billion people on the planet. She also suggested that if I wanted to narrow things down I should be on the lookout for fire-breathing, topaz-wearing archery enthusiasts, since those were all Sagittarius traits.

That Natalie wasn't a big believer in Carolina's gifts was a given — her entire worldview was predicated on empirical data and the scientific method. The strange part was that Charley wasn't a believer, either.

Actually, that wasn't strictly true. As a general rule, Charley was probably more open-minded than the average incredibly open-minded person. The problem was that I'd done some things that were sort of dangerous based on information from Carolina, and because Carolina had told me not to tell Charley, saying it would only prolong the time before I saw T.K. again, I hadn't.

Of course, when Charley found out, she'd gone ballistic. Her current feelings about Dieter paled in comparison to how she'd reacted when she learned Carolina had warned me about life-threatening dangers on the one hand and cautioned me not to mention them to Charley on the other. So Carolina wasn't Charley's favorite person these days, which was why I'd thought it best to see her on my own.

The after-work rush hour hadn't started yet, and the train

71

downtown was much less crowded than the uptown one had been that morning. We found seats between a family of chattering French tourists and a guy singing along to the Black Eyed Peas on his iPod. It wasn't the most peaceful setting, but we didn't have to worry about any of them eavesdropping.

I hadn't seen Carolina in a while, so I started by updating her on everything that had happened since we last spoke. This ended up being a complete waste of time since she was, after all, psychic and already knew just about everything I told her. But she did agree that whoever was organizing things within EAROFO was the same person as her Sagittarius. "This group that is greedy for oil, they are very bad people, and the Sagittarius is the most bad. We need to find the Sagittarius."

Then I asked what she thought about Thad as a suspect. But the main thing I learned from this was the Spanish word for weasel, and apparently it had different connotations than the English version.

"*La comadreja?*" she asked, puzzled. "Why do you call him this? This is a good animal. It kills the *ratones*. Are the *ratones* pleasing to you? No, with this Thad, I see only the math. He is like the calculator with the business of your mama, no? Plus and minus this, multiply and divide that."

"Are you saying he's not involved with what's happening in Antarctica?"

"I tell you what I see. And this Thad, I see something not right with him, but he is not part of the big group."

I was reluctant to bring up our other suspect — I was nervous about what Carolina might tell me — but I knew I had to. "Could Hunter Riley be the Sagittarius?"

"¿Cómo?"

"Hunter Riley. Quinn's father."

"Oh — the Romeo, sí? Why are you asking about his papa?"

I told her about how Hunter talked to Trip Young a lot on the phone, and how he'd been making enormous bets on the price of oil going way down, and his trip to Argentina. I also told her about one of the many unwelcome realizations I'd had recently, which was that an archer was a type of hunter.

Carolina shook her head. "No, this Hunter, he is not the Sagittarius. I am certain of it." She thought a little more. "I believe he is a Libra. Yes, he is certainly a Libra. And I do not see a Libra in the group with the Sagittarius."

I felt a flicker of relief. It wasn't like Carolina had absolved Hunter completely, but at least she didn't seem to think he was in cahoots with the others. Though now I was going to have to figure out if his being a Libra was significant in any way — I could only guess what Natalie would say about that. And none of this put my other concerns about Quinn to rest.

"But why are you not asking what you really want to be asking?" said Carolina, interrupting my thoughts.

"I was," I said.

"No, you are asking about *la comadreja* and the Libra, when you want to ask about the Quinn. But you think you should not ask because you should be playing the sport. Why do you think this? You do not like the sport."

So now I had to explain about keeping my eye on the ball, though it translated better than the weasel thing.

"That is very sensible," said Carolina. "Your mama, she is smart to tell you this. But you still worry about the Quinn?"

"It's sort of complicated. First I thought maybe he was beginning to lose interest in me, and then I found out he might be in trouble, and if he is, then I don't know if I should still like him, because if he's in trouble the way I think he's in trouble, then it means he's not the person I thought he was, which is also a problem, but I can't just stop liking him, can I?"

Carolina made an impatient noise. "In Ecuador, you would not bother about these things. You would be tired from the banana plantation. It is very hard work, you know, picking the bananas. Only in rich countries do the girls have the time to bother about what the *novio* does or does not do."

It was like she'd been talking to Charley. "But —"

She made the impatient noise again. "It is as you say. You should be with the ball. Quinn, he is confused. But he is not confused for the reasons you think."

"What's he confused about, then?"

"I do not know. He will be like the diamond soon, from the pressure, but it is not to do with you."

74

That wasn't reassuring. "But —"

"Do not bother yourself," she said with an air of finality. "That is all I know about this." Then it was like she really had been talking to Charley, because she used food to change the subject. "Now, what snacks does your auntie have in her house? I like snacks with the *televisión.*"

But when we emerged from the subway I checked my phone, and there was still no text back from Quinn.

Ten

We stopped at a deli to pick up snacks — strawberry Yoo-hoo and salt-and-vinegar potato chips for Carolina and chocolate chocolate chip Häagen-Dazs for me — and then headed for the loft. But as we rounded the corner at Hudson Street, we came face-to-face with one of the few problems I'd actually managed to forget about, at least temporarily.

Somebody was putting up condos a few blocks from Charley's, and they'd surrounded the building site with a high wall of scaffolding to protect pedestrians from construction debris. Eight and a half hours earlier, when Charley and I had passed by on our way to the subway, the plywood had been covered with peeling blue paint, graffiti, and flyers for guitar lessons and movers and dog-walkers. It had all been completely harmless.

It turned out a lot could change in eight and a half hours.

Now every available inch of the scaffolding had been transformed by Dieter harnessing the power of visual media, or whatever it was he thought he was doing. He'd used the same image, and though this version was smaller — poster-sized

76

instead of billboard-sized — he'd made up for the decrease in size with an increase in volume. Charley and I filled the entire wall, plastered in endless rows and columns for no discernible purpose.

I was speechless all over again. Carolina's reaction, on the other hand, was a lot more upbeat than Charley's and mine had been. We'd had our backs to the platform on the train downtown, so we'd missed seeing the billboards at the 51st Street station, and apparently this was her first encounter with Dieter's handiwork. "But it is spectacular," she said. "*Muy linda.* This will be yellow for you, no?"

"Why yellow?" I asked. Her tone was enthusiastic, and *linda* sounded okay, but she'd once said I felt red to her, and shortly after that someone tried to run me over.

"Yellow is good," she assured me. "Much better than red. Red is only for the Sagittarius."

Just as Carolina had promised, Charley wasn't home when we got to the loft, and she'd sent another text saying she'd be even later than she initially thought. Dieter was nowhere to be found, which was probably wise of him, and she was busy trying to figure out if there was any way to have the pictures removed from the subway. This suggested she was unaware he'd branched out from public transportation to construction, and I hoped I wouldn't be with her when she found out. In the meantime, Carolina and I didn't have to worry about her showing up in the middle of our *Bewitched* marathon.

Not that it mattered. We spent the rest of the afternoon and well into the early evening in front of the TV, curled up on opposite ends of the sofa and watching episode after episode. And while my ice cream was wholly enjoyable and the show wasn't entirely without entertainment value, the only productive thing that came out of it all was Carolina teaching herself how to twitch her nose like Samantha.

She broke it down for me — it was more of an upper lip twitch with the nose following along than an isolated nose twitch — but I still couldn't quite master it.

"Do not be envious," said Carolina. "One day you also will learn and then we will be the witches together, *sí*?" She was a lot more excited about this than I was, but for her sake I pretended I'd keep practicing until I got it right.

Otherwise, she left me nearly as directionless as I'd been before. "Your friend Rafe, he will take care of your mama," she said as she was leaving. "And the Quinn, he will be okay. You should watch the ball and think about the Sagittarius. Also, the *examen*."

"*Examen?*" I asked blankly.

She gave me her most severe look. "It will be happening soon, and you make the promise to your auntie that you will pass. You do not want to violate this promise."

Of course, in typical Carolina fashion, just because she knew about the physics quiz looming in my future didn't mean she could tell me the answers or even what questions would be on it.

So after she'd gone home, I called Natalie. I'd started taking notes in class, but I needed help decoding them. And untangling scientific mysteries was usually Natalie's idea of a good time — I didn't have to worry about imposing.

But if I'd thought it was shocking to turn a corner and see my own image repeated hundreds of times on a wall of scaffolding, I was totally unprepared for Natalie having no interest in talking about physics. It was like Mr. Dudley having no interest in talking about the Muse, or Charley having no interest in accessories.

Tonight, however, Natalie had only one thing on her mind, and that was Edward, the guy from the science fair.

They'd met up after school for coffee, and while Carolina and I were watching *Bewitched*, the two of them were sipping lattes and discovering they were soul mates. And Natalie on the subject of Edward made me on the subject of Quinn sound like Gwyneth on any subject whatsoever. It probably didn't help that she was also completely wired from the lattes.

"Did I tell you that Edward wants to go to MIT, too?" she said. "He spent his summer at Caltech doing neuromorphic systems engineering, but he spent the summer before at MIT, and he liked it better. He's considering a joint degree in nanoscience and bioengineering, but I told him about the work I've been doing in optics and now he's thinking he'll do a triple major. I can't wait for you to meet him, Delia. I invited him to the Homecoming Dance. Are you and Quinn going to go?

Because if you do, we can all hang out, Edward and me and you and Quinn."

It was hard to believe this was the same person who'd scoffed at the Homecoming Dance yesterday, much less the same person who'd been suggesting that Quinn was a criminal mastermind today. But her happiness was contagious, even over the phone, and since she agreed to meet up before school the next morning to help me prep for the physics quiz (she'd already guessed on her own we were due for one, and it wasn't like Dr. Penske had sworn Charley to secrecy or anything), I wasn't going to hold any of the other stuff against her.

The only problem was that all of Natalie's romantic giddiness just kept bringing my thoughts back to Quinn, who, according to Carolina, was confused and under pressure but not for the reasons I thought and not because of anything that had to do with me. That was promising, though I had no idea what the alternatives were to having lost interest in me or having been involved in something moronic. And either way, he still hadn't returned my text.

So after I'd paced around the loft a bit, sent a contrite belated birthday e-mail to Erin, fanned the pages of my physics notebook, done a run-through of Lady Macbeth, eaten some leftover Wiener schnitzel, organized Charley's collection of classic '80s teen movies by star (Lowe, McCarthy, Ringwald, Spader), and otherwise pretended I was being restrained and not giving way to obsessive, stalker-like behavior, I called Quinn.

I was sort of relieved when his number went straight to voice mail. It suggested maybe his battery was dead or he'd lost his phone or for some other reason hadn't even seen my text, which was infinitely better than his having seen it and ignored it. And this thought gave me the courage to do what I did next, which was to call his home phone.

It rang four times, and I was about to give up when Bea answered.

"Riley residence," she said carefully. "Beatrice Riley speaking."

"Hi, Bea. It's Delia. Is Quinn around?"

"Delia!" she cried. "Did Quinn tell you about —"

There was a fumbling noise, and she gave a muted screech as someone wrested the phone away from her. Then Oliver came on.

"This is Oliver Riley —" he started to say. But then there was another fumbling noise and an "ow!" as somebody else pulled the phone away from him.

"Both of you. Bed. Now." Fiona had her hand over the mouth of the receiver, but I could still hear her, and she sounded scary.

I'd only met Fiona a couple of times, and she hadn't seemed scary then — mostly just well-groomed — so this side of her was new. It occurred to me I should probably hang up while I still could, but before that thought could fully register, she was speaking into the phone. "Hello?"

"Hi, Fi — I mean, Mrs. Riley. Is Quinn there?"

"Who's calling, please?" she asked.

"It's Delia," I said. And then, when she didn't respond right away, I added, "Delia Truesdale." And when she still didn't respond, I added, "Quinn's friend from Prescott?"

"Yes, Delia, I know who you are," she said, and there was a bite to her tone.

"Uh, may I speak to Quinn?" I managed to get out. At this point, I was completely flummoxed.

"Quinn is unavailable at this time."

"Oh," I said. And then, since she didn't offer to take a message, I said, "Should I call back later?"

There was another long pause, and when she spoke next, her tone was so acid it practically dissolved the phone. "No, you should not."

And with that she hung up.

Eleven

I didn't sleep well that night, so I wasn't in a very good mood the next morning. Neither was Charley, though for different reasons.

It turned out that I shouldn't have worried about her seeing the scaffolding near the loft, because Dieter had been busy plastering all of the scaffolding in the city with the same posters, and she'd encountered several equally striking examples of his work on her way home. And the man himself was still missing in action, which meant we didn't know where our pictures might show up next.

I was already too upset to get more upset about this, but I was starting to wonder if I should be concerned about Charley's mental health. On the subway to school, she kept muttering under her breath about what she was going to do to Dieter if she ever found him. Of course, I was busy replaying Fiona's words over and over again in my head, and it was possible I was doing some muttering as well. The entire population of New York could have been staring and pointing at us, and a substantial chunk of it probably was, but we were both too caught up in our inner tirades to pay much attention.

So I wasn't exactly the most cheerful version of myself when I arrived at Prescott. Natalie, on the other hand, was so happy she was nearly levitating. I could almost feel my aura and hers staring at each other in confusion from opposite ends of the emotional spectrum. And though she hadn't slept well, either, in her case it was due to being too thrilled and overcaffeinated, and not because her love interest's stepmother had been overwhelmingly, crushingly mean to her.

The good news, though, at least for me, was that Natalie had used some of her excess energy to go above and beyond the call of friendship by creating a mock physics quiz I could use as a study guide. "Dr. Penske's so predictable," she said. "I guarantee whatever he hands out tomorrow will look exactly like this, just with his own inputs for the calculations."

Of course, all of Natalie's inputs seemed to involve references to Edward ("If Edward drives a car at a velocity of x and accelerates by a factor of y"), but it was so incredibly nice of her I wasn't going to tease her about it. And while I still didn't really understand why I was supposed to take the steps she said to take to solve the problems, they weren't any harder to memorize than "out damned spot."

She was walking me through everything with bemused patience — which I also credited to her euphoria since she usually walked me through things with clinically detached amazement that anyone could be so dense — when out of the corner of my eye I saw a blue Mercedes pull up to the curb.

A driver hurried from the front seat to open the door to the backseat.

Fancy chauffeur-driven cars were a pretty common sight at Prescott, so I didn't give this one much thought at first. But my heart skidded to a stop when I saw Fiona and Quinn get out.

Fiona was dressed a lot like Patience had been the other day, in a dark suit and oversized sunglasses. Quinn was in his Prescott uniform, though it seemed safe to assume the reason Fiona was there was to negotiate with the school about whether he'd be allowed to continue wearing it. Otherwise he would have arrived alone and on foot, the way he usually did.

It was only a few minutes before the first bell, so a lot of people were around, but Fiona didn't look to her right or her left as she moved briskly forward, her lips pressed into a thin, tense line. Quinn walked alongside her, and I could tell his jaw was clenched even from where Natalie and I were sitting. He, too, kept his gaze focused straight ahead, but he paused at the entrance to hold the door for Fiona, and as he did he stole a quick glance around.

For a split second, I thought he saw me, but the expression in his gray-green eyes didn't seem to change.

Then he squared his shoulders and followed Fiona inside.

The bell rang soon after that, and Natalie flitted off to her first class like Snow White singing to the birds while I trudged off like Grumpy on his way to the mines. I was glad

Fiona wasn't angry with me personally — her acid tone the night before must have had more to do with Quinn than me — but it still looked like Quinn might be in serious trouble, not that I knew how to reconcile this with what Carolina had said. And I was trying to keep my eye on the ball — I really was — but it wasn't easy when the ball kept getting buried under avalanches of distraction.

"It doesn't necessarily mean anything," Natalie said later, as we waited in the lunch line. "Mr. Seton's called in the parents of half the senior class so far."

In addition to mellowing her out, infatuation also seemed to be affecting her memory. Twenty-four hours ago she'd been certain of Quinn's pivotal involvement in the gambling ring. And while I knew she was only trying to help, somehow her attempt to reassure me was even more disconcerting.

I didn't have much interest in food, which was just as well since the chef had moved on from nation-based cuisine to color-based cuisine. The menu today was all about purple: There was coq au vin, and duck with plum sauce, and eggplant, and fig bars. It was a nice change from lamb and yogurt, but Natalie and I both went for grilled cheese anyway.

We'd barely sat down, and Natalie hadn't even had the opportunity to cut her sandwich into halves, much less quarters, when without warning a third tray clattered down next to mine. And I didn't need to look up to know who'd decided to join us. There was only one person at Prescott who considered

Fritos, pickles, and TaB to be three of the six major food groups.

"Hey," said Gwyneth, sliding into the seat adjacent to me and popping open her soda. And then, in case my existence hadn't already taken enough of a turn for the surreal, she actually joined in the conversation.

Not for the first five minutes or so, because that part was less a conversation and more a soliloquy from Natalie on whichever of Edward's virtues she'd neglected to mention as yet. This was fine with me — just because I was cranky didn't mean I should drag her down, too. I was also sort of hoping it would make Gwyneth think twice about joining us again.

But then, as Natalie wrapped up an extended description of how Edward had constructed his first telescope from plastic cups, rubber bands, and spare Power Ranger parts when he was four, Gwyneth said, "Are you talking about Edward Vargas?"

"Do you know him?" asked Natalie, startled that her path and Gwyneth's could cross in any way except by sheer accident.

Gwyneth took a long sip of TaB. "We went to camp together."

That instantly had me trying to imagine Gwyneth at camp — I mean, what kind of camp could it have been? — but nothing could tear Natalie's attention away from Edward. She'd always thought Gwyneth to be entirely a black hole, rather than just in a limited way like I was with science, but now she looked at her with fresh interest.

"What can you tell me about him?" she said. "I'm eager for additional data points."

Gwyneth crunched a Frito. "He's sort of a player, isn't he?"

Across the table, Natalie flinched. "A player? What do you mean, a player?"

Gwyneth shrugged. "You know. Like, a player."

"Are you saying he goes out with a lot of different people?" I asked.

"Uh-huh," said Gwyneth, washing down the Frito with more soda. "He's supposed to be a major serial."

"What's a serial?" I asked, since Natalie had been struck temporarily mute.

"Like, a guy who'll be really serious about one person, but then he dumps that person after a week and moves on to the next person, which will last a week, and then he dumps her and moves on to the next person. And so on. A serial."

"Are you absolutely sure?" I asked Gwyneth. "We're talking about the same Edward Vargas?"

"He goes to Dalton, right?" she asked Natalie.

Natalie nodded, still mute.

Gwyneth shrugged again. "Same guy."

Natalie's face had gone so white it was starting to scare me. She was even paler than Gwyneth. Meanwhile, Gwyneth seemed unaware of having single-handedly reduced Natalie's entire world to jagged shards of dashed hope.

"It might just be rumors," I rushed to tell Natalie before she could pass out or anything. "You know how little things can spin out of control. Somebody hears something and tells someone else and the next thing you know there's a story out there that's totally different from reality. It's not real evidence. It's hearsay."

"Hearsay," Natalie repeated softly.

Then she said it again, more firmly this time, and it was like the word suddenly switched on her inner prosecutor.

The color came rushing back to her face, and she pushed her tray to the side and grabbed a pad of graph paper and a mechanical pencil from her bag. "I want the details," she said to Gwyneth. "Names, dates, known associates, suspected accomplices — anything you can give me about this allegedly serial behavior."

And it was like we'd accidentally stumbled onto Gwyneth's secret area of expertise. She reeled off who had done what to whom and when and how they'd done it like she had a database stored in her head. It was also the only topic I'd ever seen animate her. Her face actually moved more than the bare minimum required for words to pass from her lips as she told Natalie everything she'd ever heard about Edward Vargas.

Which turned out to be a lot. According to Gwyneth, Edward had been cutting a swath through the city's female population since the sixth grade. I couldn't imagine how he'd

89

found time to do all of the things she said he'd done when he was so busy with MIT and Caltech and everything, but apparently he was an accomplished multitasker.

When Gwyneth was finally tapped out, Natalie leaned back in her chair and studied the paper before her, shaking her head in stunned disbelief. "The data here is so inconsistent with what I observed on an empirical basis when we met. He seemed so genuine."

"What are you going to do?" I asked.

Even Gwyneth was curious enough to ask. "Yeah. What?"

"I don't know," said Natalie. Her voice sounded strangely unfamiliar to me, and I realized it was because I'd never heard her be indecisive before.

When she spoke again, though, it was with her usual crisp certainty. "But I'm sure I'll think of something."

Twelve

Sadly, while Gwyneth was full of information about anything to do with people hooking up in Manhattan, selected parts of the Hamptons, Palm Beach, and Aspen, she was useless when it came to more urgent matters like what might have happened to Quinn in Mr. Seton's office that morning.

But that didn't stop her from thinking we were better friends now than ever before, and when Mr. Dudley canceled class, citing the number of absent students and an unspecified conflict, which probably meant he had an audition, she followed me up to the library without asking where I was going or why.

Prescott's Upper School was housed in two adjacent brick-and-stone town houses, and the library stretched across what had once been the attics of both buildings. Now the space was bright and modern, with skylights in the sloping ceilings and study carrels tucked in among the bookshelves. It would've been a pleasant place just to hang out and read, but Gwyneth peeled off without comment and disappeared into the stacks, and I made directly for the row of computers lining one wall.

I probably could've spent the unexpected free period studying for my physics quiz, but it seemed only fair I should be able to use at least part of the time to focus on the Sagittarius, like Carolina had suggested. The other alternative was fretting more about Quinn, and I knew exactly what Carolina would have to say about that.

There wasn't a lot of public information available on EAROFO — it didn't have its own Web site or handy MySpace page for those of us trying to figure out what sinister plots it might have under way. The only source I'd found so far was an online directory of Washington, D.C.-based lobbying organizations that provided the names and titles of EAROFO's board members. Now I returned to the Web page and printed it out for a better look.

There were twelve board members in total, and I studied the list for what felt like the millionth time, hoping maybe I'd generate a fresh insight or new lead. But I already knew about Trip Young from Navitaco, and the eleven others were still nothing more than names on a piece of paper. The accompanying photos showed ten white men, one black man, and a white woman, all dressed in nearly identical business suits and entirely unremarkable except for how uniformly old and stuffy they looked.

Printing out the list and checking it again took less than two minutes, so then I started Googling the individual board members. I'd done this before, too, a couple of weeks ago, and had only turned up links to the Web sites for their respective companies and the occasional reference to something more personal

92

but equally unrevealing, like a country club tennis championship or a charity gala.

Nothing had changed since the last time I'd tried, but it was frustrating to get the same results anyway. So to narrow things down a bit, I searched for each name with Thad Wilcox, and then, to be fair, with Hunter Riley as well. Carolina had told me neither was part of the group that was "greedy for oil," but it wasn't like she'd definitely said they were innocent, either. She'd even said that there was something "not right" about Thad.

And Google did return a bunch of hits. Which was exciting until I realized none of them was particularly incriminating.

For example, Thad had played in an amateur golf tournament years ago with Victor Perkins, the chairman of Perkins Oil, but so had tons of other people, and both he and Sam Arquero, the head of Arquero Energy, were active in the Princeton alumni association — again, along with a cast of thousands. Hunter spoke on a panel with Trip Young at a recent Wall Street conference, but I already knew they were acquainted. He'd also served on a fund-raising committee for an adult literacy program, and so had Anthony Kaplan, the CEO of Energex, but there wasn't any overlap between the periods during which they'd each been actively involved.

So it wasn't like I was turning up lots of evidence documenting close ties between Thad or Hunter and anyone at EAROFO. Not that I really expected to, but at this point I would have welcomed any lead, however tenuous or remote. Otherwise, I felt like I was sitting around, powerless, as I waited for Rafe to return from South America or Charley to dig up another random "source" or Carolina to have another illuminating dream.

I was closing down the Web browser when I heard my phone quietly buzzing from the depths of my book bag. The librarian was at the far end of the room, at his desk and with his back to me, so I decided it would be safe to slip the phone out and check messages.

My immediate thought — complete with another missed heartbeat — was that Quinn had finally texted, and I tried not to be disappointed when I saw the only person I'd heard from was Charley. Of course, I was even more disappointed when I read her message:

> please don't hate me
> can't make dinner w/ WW
> absolutely legit reasons — really!
> go w/Monkeys after school
> take taxi home — make sure driver sees u inside
> have I mentioned please don't hate me?

Charley sometimes called Patience the Wicked Witch of the Upper East Side. She also referred to Gwyneth and Grey as the Flying Monkeys. Of Jeremy, Patience's husband, Charley just said, "They're perfect for each other. Which should tell you a lot."

I'd completely forgotten we were supposed to have dinner at Patience's apartment. This had probably been willful self-delusion on my part — family fun at the Truesdale-Babbitt household wasn't high on the list of things I wanted to do that evening, or ever for that matter. It also didn't help that I'd already had enough quality time with Gwyneth to last for the next several decades, but it looked like I was in for more, and Charley wouldn't be there as a buffer.

I was about to write back asking for details on the "absolutely legit reasons" — Patience would be sure to ask — when my phone buzzed with another new text.

This one wasn't from Quinn, either, though I was starting to wonder if skipping heartbeats so frequently added up to a work-out of sorts. It was just an afterthought from Charley:

p.s. — might want to avoid bus shelters

Which, even for Charley, made no sense. She'd told me in her first text to take a taxi. So I was about to write back to that when she beat me to it again:

p.p.s. — also ice cream trucks

Which made even less sense. She knew perfectly well I preferred my ice cream in pint form — the soft-serve cones and Good Humor bars the trucks sold were only for when things got desperate and there wasn't a grocery store or deli nearby with a decent freezer section —

"What're you doing?"

Gwyneth's voice at my shoulder was so unexpected I almost dropped the phone, and my heart skipped yet another beat, this time because I was startled and not due to a jolt of hopeful anticipation. I'd liked the hopeful anticipation better.

"Texting Charley," I said. "She can't make dinner."

"My mom will flip. But I was asking about the old people," she said, tapping the printout on the table before me.

"Oh. That. It's just some research. For a project."

"What kind of project?" she asked.

"For, uh —" I tried to think of a class Gwyneth would know nothing about. "It's for Latin."

"Latin?"

"Sure," I said, trying to sound like a list of oil company executives was precisely the sort of thing a person would need to research for Latin class. Mostly I was wondering why Gwyneth had chosen this moment of all moments to discover her curiosity.

She peered down at the paper. "Does EAROFO mean something in Latin?"

96

Not that I was aware of, but if that's what she wanted to think, it was fine with me. "It means, uh —"

But before I could think of a suitable lie, the bell rang to signal the end of the school day, and it also seemed to shut down Gwyneth's interest. She hoisted her Prada bag over her shoulder and turned toward the door. "Ready?" she asked.

I moved to follow her, too relieved that she'd dropped the subject of EAROFO to process the way she'd said "ready." Like there was no question of us not leaving together, and, even scarier, like that's how it would always be.

A chill went through me. I had no idea what the new black might be, but one thing was becoming all too clear: Delia was the new Grey.

Thirteen

Patience and her family lived only a few blocks from Prescott, so Gwyneth and I walked to their apartment after school. At least, I walked. Gwyneth sort of ambled. But those few short blocks were all it took for Charley's last two texts to get a lot less cryptic.

Because first we passed the shelter at a bus stop, and Charley and I were splashed across the side. At this point, I was starting to feel numb to the whole thing — I mean, bus shelters were a logical progression for Dieter as he moved on from subways and scaffolding, and mostly I was glad we hadn't shown up on an actual bus. Somehow the idea of my face rolling up and down the avenues was more than I could take.

But it was like that thought called up what I saw next, and it almost had me wishing for a bus instead. Because right on East 79th Street, parked in a prime spot for catching tourists on their way to and from Central Park and the Metropolitan Museum of Art, was an ice cream truck. And I didn't know how Dieter had pulled it off, but the big cartoon drawing of the Mister Softee man on the side of the truck, the drawing with the jaunty red bow tie and ice-cream cone hat, was gone, replaced by Charley and me.

The strangest part was that Gwyneth was oblivious. She didn't notice the bus shelter or the truck, even though we came within twenty feet of each. And when we passed some scaffolding at 79th and Park — scaffolding Dieter had most definitely not spared — she stayed oblivious. I wasn't complaining or anything, but it was weird.

The apartment was quiet when we arrived, and since Patience was the only person in the household who ever made any noise, I decided she probably wasn't home yet. Neither Jeremy nor Grey seemed to be around, either, as Gwyneth led me down one of the many hallways off the foyer and into her room. Like the rest of the place, it was decorated in high-end preppy, with a four-poster bed and chintz-covered pillows.

I hadn't really thought about how we'd spend the time between school and dinner, but I guess I assumed there'd be some studying. In spite of how little work I'd been doing, Prescott was a demanding place, and I couldn't imagine Patience letting her kids shirk their academic responsibilities. But instead Gwyneth picked up a remote control, and with the press of a button the large mirror over the bureau transformed itself into a TV.

"How about this one?" she asked, scrolling through a list of recorded programs and pausing at something called *Kinkajou Kribs*.

I'd thought I'd seen a new side of Gwyneth at lunch, but I was totally unprepared for her love of small mammals. We watched kinkajous, meerkats, Alpine marmots, hoary marmots, and various other creatures cavorting across the screen, and while I admit it was kind of addictive, Gwyneth was entranced. She laughed aloud at the antics of a crested porcupine and cooed over baby two-toed sloths. And the tragedy of it all was that Charley would never believe me without physical proof, and I worried Gwyneth would take it the wrong way if I tried to snap a picture.

Anyhow, everyone else must have arrived home while we were watching TV, and at precisely half past seven Patience's voice rang out over the intercom summoning us to dinner. Gwyneth reluctantly pressed another button, the screen turned into a mirror again, and we went down another hallway and into the dining room.

The first thing I'd learned about Patience was that her favorite adjective was "appropriate," and in this context it seemed to mean greeting me with an air kiss to each cheek and making sure the butler or manservant or whatever you were supposed to call him didn't stint on the tilapia or Swiss chard. Meanwhile, Gwyneth — at least, I assumed it had been Gwyneth, because I didn't know who else would have done it — must have put a word in with the guy, too, because my water glass was filled with the same mixture of vodka and vodka that was her own drink of choice at family dinners. I probably should've been touched by this demonstration of cousinly affection, but it only made me more nervous about whatever role she envisioned me playing in her life going forward.

Especially since the conversation at dinner suggested Grey's absence from Prescott really might turn permanent.

"Not a word from you, buster," Patience snapped when he appeared at the table. This seemed unnecessary — it wasn't like Grey ever spoke anyway — and hearing her call him "buster" had me reaching for my water to hide the giggling fit it inspired, which led to a choking fit after I'd taken a big gulp and discovered what was actually in my glass. Gwyneth's expression was blank as she reached over and pounded me on the back.

"Pass the salt," said Jeremy from his end of the table.

"Cordelia, have you heard what my idiot son and his idiot friends have been up to?" Patience asked me. I wasn't sure how to answer that, but fortunately Patience was fully capable of carrying on a conversation without anyone else's involvement. "I've spent the last forty-eight hours trying to prevent him from being expelled, which would be significantly easier if Prescott's endowment weren't larger than the gross domestic product of certain small developing countries and we could buy his way back in. Though our money might be better spent buying his way into a lesser institution. I'm thinking military school would be a superb choice for addressing his character flaws. Perhaps in one of those places like Nebraska or South Dakota where they also have to herd sheep and plow. Do you have any thoughts on military school, Cordelia?"

I knew what Charley would say, and it had to do with the movie *Taps*, which she'd made me watch as part of a "Sean Penn: The Early Years" triple feature that also included *Fast Times at Ridgemont High* and *Bad Boys*. But I just said, "I'm afraid not, sorry." And then, in an attempt to make sure the evening wasn't a complete waste, I tried to change the topic to something I really did want to discuss. "I was wondering, have you talked to Thad Wilcox since he was here last week?"

Patience wasn't any happier with Thad than she was with her son. "Hardly," she said, slicing into her tilapia like she wished it was Thad's jugular. "After I refused to sign those papers, he stormed out in a most unprofessional manner. I must say, Cordelia, I do not trust that man, and I will not stand silently by as he attempts to usurp your rightful position. He will rue the day he crossed me. I've left several messages with his office in Palo Alto, and his assistant says he's out of the country, but I don't see how that precludes his returning calls. She claims he's unreachable, which is preposterous. There's not a single inch of the planet these days without cellular service or Wi-Fi."

I doubted Patience had ever stood silently by as anything occurred, but I was much less concerned than she was about being usurped since I knew T.K. would fix it all when she returned. No, mostly I was stuck on the part about Thad being out of the country and unreachable.

Because it wasn't true that every inch of the planet had cellular service and Wi-Fi. For example, I knew for a fact there were parts of Chilean Patagonia where the communications infrastructure was completely primitive.

"Did Thad's assistant happen to at least say which continent —" I was asking Patience when the butler guy leaned down to whisper something in her ear.

If she was surprised by what he said, it was impossible to tell, because the top half of her face stayed perfectly immobile — thanks to her dermatologist, Patience couldn't have moved her eyebrows even if she'd wanted to. "Have her brought up and shown into the small sitting room," she told him.

Then she turned back to the table. "How odd. Fiona Riley is here."

There were eight million people in New York City, but in certain ways it functioned like a tiny little village. So it wasn't a shock to learn that Patience and Fiona were close enough to drop in on each other unexpectedly — they'd probably hung out at a ton of Prescott parents' events over the years, not to mention the whole Upper East Side benefit/Pilates/Bergdorf's circuit.

It also wasn't a shock to discover that the only person in the Truesdale-Babbitt household who seemed to care about family dinner was Patience, because as soon as she left the dining room Jeremy and Grey vanished, too.

I was thinking this meant an early reprieve for me, and I was already planning what I'd do in the taxi on the way home. First, I needed to let Rafe and Charley know Thad might be trying to retrace T.K.'s footsteps himself. Then I'd take advantage of Fiona's absence from home to try calling Quinn. One of the many things I'd been hoping was that she'd taken away his phone and computer privileges, which would explain the continued radio silence on his end.

But as I moved to follow Jeremy and Grey out of the dining room, Gwyneth silently gestured for me to wait. I opened my mouth to protest — a person can watch just so much Animal Planet — but she shook her head, holding a finger to her lips. Then, as soon as we were alone, she grabbed my arm and led me through the swinging door into the kitchen, through a pantry, down another hallway, and into a supply closet, closing the door after us.

"Wh —" I started to ask.

"Shh," she whispered. "Listen."

And when I did, I could hear Patience and Fiona as clearly as if they were in the closet with us. As my eyes adjusted to the dark, I could make out a thin glimmer of light shining through a register grate set in the wall. The sitting room must have been right on the other side, and the voices were traveling through the grate along with the lamplight.

"— sorry to intrude," Fiona was saying. The acid that had been in her voice when she'd spoken to me was gone, and her words came out in a high-pitched, stressed-out rush. "I would've called but Bea and Oliver always manage to overhear anything that happens in the house and then I think I lost my cell phone — I can't find it anywhere, I must have left it in another handbag or maybe at the trainer's — you know I wouldn't have just shown up with no notice if I weren't at my wits' end."

"So Quinn's been implicated in the gambling venture?" said Patience, sounding extra crisp next to Fiona's near hysteria.

"Not officially, not yet. Francis Seton says he's certain Quinn knows more than he's letting on, but Quinn won't admit it and he also won't deny it — he only says he's not at liberty to comment, like a lawyer told him to say that, and I can't convince him to cooperate. He refuses to listen to me. I'm only his stepmother, after all — I can't force him to do anything — and he still has issues after everything that happened with Paula, not that she'd be any help in a situation like this."

"But why are you dealing with it at all?" asked Patience. "Why isn't Hunter handling everything?"

"Hunter!" said Fiona, her voice rising another two octaves. "Hunter's supposed to be in Argentina, and usually he'd be on the first plane back if anything happened to one of the kids, but he hasn't responded to a single message. And when I tried to reach him through his secretary, she said he'd told her he was on vacation. I've never been so humiliated in my life — now his entire office knows I have no idea where my husband is. And even if he is in Argentina, he lied about it being a business trip,

105

and if he lied about that, then I'm not sure I want to know what else he's lied about."

Fiona's voice caught, and I could almost picture her pretty face crumpling, though it was possible she went to Patience's dermatologist, too, in which case it wouldn't crumple at all.

"Why don't we get you some hot tea? Or I have a better idea — how about a nice, stiff drink?" suggested Patience, in a more soothing tone than I'd ever heard her use before, though it seemed like if she was going to use it on anyone, she might have started with her theoretically orphaned niece.

Then their voices faded away as they left the room together.

Fourteen

Gwyneth and I returned to her bedroom without discussing what we'd heard, and she didn't show any interest in rehashing it in private, either. Before I'd even picked up my jacket and book bag she was tuned in to Animal Planet and rapt all over again, though she might have waved as I left. A couple of her fingers seemed to flutter.

I didn't run into anyone else as I left the apartment. From behind one closed door I could hear a baseball game on TV, and from another I could hear a murmur of voices that must have been Patience and Fiona. I probably should've stopped to say thank you and good-bye to Patience, but I had no desire to encounter Fiona in the flesh. Instead I let myself out and took the elevator down to the lobby.

Outside it had started to rain, and the doorman hailed a taxi for me, holding his umbrella over us both for the short distance from building to curb. The cabdriver was on his headset, speaking in Caribbean-accented French and barely pausing long enough for me to give him Charley's address before returning to his conversation. I didn't mind — I wanted some time to myself to put my thoughts in order.

But first I had a couple of pressing items to take care of, beginning with Thad. I quickly composed a text and shot it off to Charley and Rafe:

Simon might be visiting Madge's neighbor

We hadn't bothered to create a code name for Chile, and I hoped that "neighbor" would be self-explanatory, since Chile bordered Argentina on the map. But while I was pretty sure Rafe would know what I meant, sometimes Charley could come up with bizarre answers to basic questions.

Next I tried Quinn's house. But Fiona must have switched off the Rileys' home phone, because it didn't even ring before a voice mail announcement came on. And after the previous night's conversation, I wasn't about to leave a recording for the entire household to hear.

With all of that done, or at least partially done and partially attempted in an incredibly unsatisfying manner, I leaned back against the seat and tried to sort through everything I'd learned, not that I really knew where to begin or what to make of anything.

For starters there was Thad, out of the country and unreachable. If he was a normal person, that could mean a million different things, but this was a guy I'd never seen without his BlackBerry — he probably slept with it on his pillow and called it a secret pet name, like Pookie or Shnookums. Nor was he the type to suddenly drop everything for a nice holiday in a location so remote it lacked decent cellular service. It was impossible not to worry that he'd somehow found out that T.K. was still alive and had picked up her trail in Patagonia.

And I knew that trail would lead to Argentina, which brought me to Hunter, who was already there. After what I'd heard from Fiona, I couldn't think he might be on a harmless business trip — if it was business, his office would have known about it. As a general rule, people who were up to good things didn't deliberately mislead everyone in their lives about where they were going and why they were going there, even if they did take those people to Chuck E. Cheese before they left. So this latest revelation was less than reassuring.

And thinking about Hunter and his lies only kept bringing me back to Quinn and whatever it was he wasn't saying. No matter how I tried to spin it, his whole situation sounded bleak. And while I knew I was supposed to be keeping my eye on the ball and starring in my own movie and not obsessing, what Fiona had said about Quinn's mother, Paula, made my heart go out to him completely.

Quinn's parents split up when he was seven, and there'd been an ugly custody battle, with Hunter saying a lot of things about Paula being an unfit mother and mentally unstable. Paula had pretty much disappeared from Quinn's life after that, but he still felt guilty about how he hadn't been able to protect her, even though he'd only been a little kid at the time.

And now he was going through something awful, and it was hard not to think that in a way, with his mother out of commission and his father up to no good, he was more of an orphan at that moment than I'd ever been.

Even though it was well past rush hour, traffic was heavy, and the rain made it worse. The wet pavement reflected the brake lights of the cars in front of us as the taxi crawled south on Park Avenue, and thick fog shrouded the tops of the office towers in midtown.

We reached Union Square just as a signal turned red, and as we sat waiting for it to change, my eyes landed on the enormous digital clock mounted on a building on the south end of the square, its numbers glowing yellow-orange against the dark of the facade. As clocks went, it was a complicated version. On the left it counted up the hours and minutes and seconds that had elapsed since midnight, and on the right it counted down the hours and minutes and seconds remaining until the next midnight. The digits came together in the middle in a blur of neon milliseconds.

But watching the time flash by, I realized it wasn't yet six o'clock on the West Coast, and there might be a very easy way to answer at least one of my questions.

I'd been relying on Patience to get a handle on what was going on with Thad. And that had been okay when I'd thought

Thad was safely behind his desk in California. But the circumstances had changed — I needed information now. I also had access to people at T.K.'s company in a way Patience never would, because so many of them had watched me grow up. Somebody there would be able to tell me what Thad was up to, and I knew exactly where to start.

Brett Fitzgerald was my mother's assistant, and her extension was programmed into my phone. With a pang I realized it hadn't occurred to me to wonder what had happened to her in the wake of T.K.'s disappearance — it wasn't as bad as spacing on Erin's birthday, but Brett had been part of my life since I was a toddler. I just hoped she hadn't left the company now that T.K. was gone.

And for once I was in luck, because she was still at the same extension, and she answered right away.

"Delia!" she cried. "I was just thinking about you, baby. How're you doing?"

Brett might have been one of the people who'd watched me grow up, but she still called me "baby," though that was probably only fair since she'd also made sure that T.K. had been present for every major event in my life, from my kindergarten graduation to the day I'd finally gotten my braces off. And I felt another pang when I heard the concern in her tone. Like most people from home, she expected me to be in a delicate state, since in theory I'd recently lost my mother. It wasn't like I could let her know what was really going on, either, which just made the guilt multiply.

But as soon as I could steer the conversation away from me and back to Brett, I almost forgot about the guilt, because it turned out that with my mother gone, Brett had been reassigned to another executive, and that executive was Thad. Not that she was happy about it.

"He actually keeps track of how long I take for lunch with a stopwatch. A stopwatch! And when I'm back in fifty-nine minutes, I don't hear about being early, but a second over sixty minutes and it's like I've been out selling company secrets. We're all relieved on the days when he's not in the office."

Which was the perfect opening. "Is he there now?" I asked, even though I knew he wasn't.

"No, thank God for small favors. He's been gone for over a week. First he was in New York — you saw him there, right? — and instead of coming back here, he suddenly calls demanding I clear his calendar and book him on the next flight to Santiago."

On some level, that was precisely what I'd been expecting to hear, but that didn't mean it wasn't a shock. "Santiago as in Chile?" I asked, just to be sure.

"Uh-huh. And then Mr. I-Can't-Last-Five-Minutes-Without-Checking-Messages goes completely off the grid before calling this afternoon and yelling about how he needs to get on the next flight from Santiago to Buenos Aires."

Brett kept talking, about how TrueTech didn't have any customers in Chile or Argentina so she couldn't understand Thad's sudden interest in the region. Of course, she didn't know the whole story. Not that I did, either, but I knew enough of it to wonder if now would be a good time to start seriously panicking.

After all, pretty much every EAROFO member company had an outpost in Buenos Aires. Hunter was in Buenos Aires. Thad was in Buenos Aires. And T.K. was in Buenos Aires.

At least, I told myself, Rafe was there, too, and maybe he really did have a black belt. He'd make sure my mother stayed safe, even with the various sharks circling around her.

Except as soon as I hung up with Brett, a text came through from Charley.

Madge's neighbor?
Rafe on plane back; landing NY in AM

Which left T.K. without even the non-Rock-like presence of Rafe. And I knew she was in hiding and everything, and that Mark guy was probably with her, and there were thirteen million other people in the greater Buenos Aires area to shield them, but panicking seemed increasingly like a reasonable option.

Only twenty-four hours ago, Carolina had told me I had nothing to worry about. Rafe would take care of T.K., neither

Thad nor Hunter was the Sagittarius, and Quinn was under a lot of pressure but not for the reasons I thought.

But every single thing I'd learned since then threw every single thing she'd told me into question.

And now I had no idea what to think.

Fifteen

I waited up for Charley, even though she didn't get back until after midnight. It turned out she'd spent her entire day alternating between trying to locate Dieter and trying to figure out if he'd been harnessing the power of visual media in ways we had yet to discover. And while both his whereabouts and his rationale for papering the entire city with our images remained a mystery, she had learned he'd been using their production company's credit card to pay for it all, from the billboards in the subway to Mister Softee. Unfortunately, she'd also learned he'd already maxed out the credit limit, which meant she couldn't stop him by canceling the card.

So she wasn't in the greatest mood to start with — when she walked in she didn't even pause to put her bag down but just made directly for the freezer and pulled out every pint of ice cream we had — and none of the developments I shared with her did anything to improve her spirits, though she tried to act like everything was under control for my sake.

"It will be fine," she said. "Your mother's in a safe place, and Mark is with her. And when Rafe's flight lands tomorrow morning he'll be able to give them a heads-up to be on the lookout for Thad along with Hunter and everyone else."

But the way she didn't comment on Gwyneth's love of Animal Planet or her secret eavesdropping closet combined with how she insisted I finish off the rest of the double chocolate peanut butter fudge, which I knew was her favorite, told me she was far more concerned than she let on, and that didn't exactly help with my own anxiety levels.

For the second night in a row, I didn't sleep well. You probably couldn't even call what I did sleeping — mostly it was a lot of staring up at the ceiling while my thoughts raced around in a circle, skidding from one worry to the next and then around again after they'd completed a full circuit. But just as the sky was starting to get a little less black outside the window, I must have drifted off, because when the phone rang the noise jerked me awake.

It wasn't my cell phone, or Charley's, either. It was the landline out in the main room of the loft, the one only telemarketers and Patience ever used. And under normal circumstances, I wouldn't have budged — Charley could sleep through a symphony of jackhammers in her bedroom, so it wasn't like the ringing would disturb her — but with everything that was going on I was out of bed and rushing to answer it without thinking twice about why anyone would be calling at such a strange time.

In the semidark, it took me a couple of rings to locate the handset on the kitchen counter, and I stubbed my toe in the process, so I had to hop around silently cursing for another couple of rings before I could pick up. "Hello?"

"Why are you not trusting what I tell you?" a voice demanded. "It is very discourteous."

The green numbers on the microwave clock read 5:13 A.M., and I must have been more asleep than I'd realized, because it took me a moment to place the voice and remember the other person who sometimes called on this line. "Carolina?"

"I do not know why I bother to tell you things when you do not listen. In my country, the children have the respect for the elders."

Apparently she was referring to herself as the elder and me as the child in this situation, which seemed like a stretch given she was only a few years older than I was, but it seemed unwise to point that out when she was already so riled up. "I do have the respect —"

"You ask for my help and then you disregard what I say. And you do very little preparation for the *examen*. You spend your time watching the TV with the sleepy cousin."

"But —"

"I am not always knowing all there is to be knowing, but what I am knowing is always correct, is that not true?"

"Yes, but —"

"I will still tell you what I must tell you, but I do not want you to be doubting me. It is very ungrateful."

"I don't mean to be ungrate —"

"*La Morena.* We did not talk of La Morena before, we are thinking she is not important. But I see now, she is very important."

"What's a *morena*?"

"A lady with brown hair. Hers is like mine but not so long, and also she has the tan coat with the belt, *cómo se dice*, the trench coat, *sí*? She is in my dream, and when I wake, I know that she is very dangerous. Very red. It is possible she is the Sagittarius she is so red."

"But —"

"That is all I am knowing in this moment. I will tell you more when I see more. But be keeping your eye on La Morena. Now I must go. I do not want to be late for sunrise yoga."

I returned the handset to its cradle and limped back to my room — my big toe was still throbbing from where I'd smashed it into the leg of a chair — but I didn't bother trying to get to sleep again. Instead, I went to sit on the broad sill of the window, watching as the sky turned from charcoal to a watery gray and thinking through what Carolina had said.

I knew exactly who Carolina meant when she talked about "La Morena," not that I knew the woman's name or anything else about her beyond what she looked like. But this woman was the only person I could think of who fit Carolina's description, with brown hair down to her shoulders and a trench coat, though sometimes she pinned her hair up and she didn't always wear the trench coat.

All along, we'd assumed she was merely another EAROFO puppet, like the "researchers" on the *Polar Star*. It hadn't occurred to us that she might be a puppet master in her own right, pulling the strings herself. But now, as I added everything up, I realized it made perfect sense.

I'd seen this woman on a total of five occasions. The first time was a couple of weeks ago, when she'd walked past on the sidewalk in front of Prescott as I sat talking to Natalie before school. I'd seen her again on the afternoon of that same day, when I was with Quinn in Central Park, and then a few days later, in the ladies' room of the theater where Quinn took me to see an off-off-Broadway production of *Romeo and Juliet*, though I didn't put her together at that point with the woman on the sidewalk and in the park.

It wasn't until the day after that, when I'd seen her leaving Navitaco's offices, that I recognized her as the same person I'd been seeing everywhere else. And that had been on a Monday, and on the following Tuesday, she'd called my name and beckoned from across the street, hoping to lure me into the path of an SUV hurtling full-speed in my direction.

Looking back on the whole thing, I was surprised we'd all managed to pass her over as a serious suspect. We'd assumed that whoever was really orchestrating things would delegate the dirty work, like tailing me or conspiring to commit vehicular homicide, the way they'd delegated the dirty work of doing away with my mother.

Meanwhile, because we knew so little about her, we hadn't tried to track her down ourselves — there was no obvious place to start. It wasn't like with the original captain of the *Polar Star*, where presumably T.K. would be able to give us a name and other background information. This woman was entirely anonymous.

It didn't help that she looked so normal. She'd blended in perfectly everywhere I'd seen her, and there was nothing about her appearance to suggest she was evil to the core. If anything, she was sort of pretty, about Charley's age, with shiny hair and pert features and cat-shaped eyes, though Charley would have found her fashion sense lacking. Charley wore a trench coat sometimes, too, but hers was zebra striped.

And if trying to track this woman down before had seemed hard, now it seemed impossible. She'd completely stopped following me after the Range Rover incident — at least, I hadn't seen her recently, and I'd actually been on the lookout. And while I knew that was probably something to be thankful for, I couldn't help but worry about what she might be up to in her spare time now that she wasn't busy shadowing me, and I also wished she'd left us with more to go on before she'd decided to leave me alone.

It would have been a lot easier if La Morena had let Charley style her. Because even if she was still in New York — which was a big if, since Buenos Aires seemed to exert a magnetic pull on evildoers — there must have been tens of thousands of other women with brown hair and beige trench coats around, and hundreds of thousands when you factored in the greater tristate area.

But there were probably only a handful of brown-haired women wearing zebra stripes.

Sixteen

That morning was cool and damp, and despite what I'd been told about New York being such a diverse and individualistic place, it seemed like every single person on the subway was wearing a beige trench coat.

Not Charley, of course. She was wearing her zebra print, but between the weather and our rotten moods, the striped material looked somehow less bold, like it would rather have been an area rug than a coat, so it could lie inside on a nice quiet floor instead of having to traipse around the city in the drizzle and mist.

Meanwhile, I was wearing my uniform, but it wasn't by choice. I'd tried to convince Charley with what little coherence I had left after another sleepless night that today would be a really good day to skip school. And it wasn't just that I wanted to be conveniently absent for Dr. Penske's pop quiz, though that would have been an added plus. Instead, I wanted to go to the airport to meet Rafe's flight, so he could tell us whatever news he had, we could tell him ours, and then he could return to Argentina and make sure none of the various bad guys converging on Buenos Aires could get anywhere near my mother.

Charley, however, refused to be persuaded by any of my extremely valid arguments. "I made a promise to Dr. Penske that you would pass this quiz, and you can't pass if you're not there to take it. And he pledged scout's honor. I can't renege."

"But you're not the scout. He is."

"If one party of an agreement is a scout, that automatically binds every party of the agreement to the scouting code of honor."

"I bet you don't even know what the scouting code of honor is," I said.

"No, but I think it's safe to assume honoring one's promises is part of it," said Charley. "And also helping old people across the street."

After some back-and-forth, we reached a compromise. I'd stay at Prescott until physics was over, but Charley would come up with an excuse so I could leave after and we'd go meet Rafe together.

Once that was settled, Charley insisted on spending the trip uptown trying to help me study. Unfortunately, I'd made the mistake of telling her how memorizing Natalie's directions was like memorizing lines for a play, and Charley felt we should do a dramatic reading of the study guide, right there on the subway. At this point, we'd pretty much given up worrying about people staring — in fact, Charley's attitude was that we might as well embrace it — so we ran through the mock quiz and everyone around us watched like we were insane. It was completely morti-fying, though I had to admit it was useful for refreshing my memory.

"Who is this Edward person?" she asked after we'd finished the final Edward-referencing question and acknowledged the applause from our audience.

"Some guy from Dalton. Natalie thought he was her soul mate, but then Gwyneth told her he's a player, so now Natalie's figuring out if she can sue him for fraud or misrepresentation or something like that."

"Natalie the genius prodigy is taking relationship advice from one of the Monkeys?"

"It wasn't really advice — more like data. Natalie did her own analysis and interpretation."

"That's it," said Charley. "I know what I'm doing after Dieter is dead. There's clearly a massive demand for my services."

"Which services?"

"Young love advisory services. The youth of America need me. They'll be so much less mopey and whiny once I'm finished with them, and the entire country will be grateful. I'm seeing the Presidential Medal of Freedom and possibly even a Nobel Peace Prize in my future. What do you think?"

"Definitely the Nobel," I said.

When I arrived at Prescott, Natalie was waiting out front, holding an umbrella patterned with the Copernican model of the solar system (at least, that's what it said on the umbrella). "I was hoping I'd catch you before school started," she said.

I assumed she wanted to cram in more physics prep — she probably didn't trust that I'd done any on my own, which wasn't so far from the truth. "I did study," I said, trying not to sound too defensive. "Really."

"That's great," she said, like she was proud of me. "You'll find it makes the quiz-taking experience far less traumatic. But that's not what I wanted to talk to you about."

She pulled out her iPhone and began dialing into voice mail. "This came in last night, but I had the phone turned off — the cellular signal interferes with the experiments I'm running on nanowave frequencies in a fixed optic environment — so I only received the message this morning, when I switched the phone back on."

"Is it from Edward?" I asked, thinking maybe she had another data point and wanted my help with the analysis.

"No," she said, with a noncommittal shrug. "I'm still working on that. Here."

Natalie handed me the phone, and an automated voice announced she had one saved message, sent yesterday at 9:34 P.M. from a local caller, though I didn't recognize the number.

Then another voice, a real one, began speaking, and after a two-and-a-half-day absence, it was good for a quick spasm of brain paralysis.

Uh, Natalie. Hi. This is Quinn. Quinn Riley. From Prescott.

I felt the uncontrollable smile spreading across my face. Did Quinn really not understand he needed no introduction? Everyone at Prescott knew exactly who he was, from the littlest kid in pre-K all the way up to the most ancient member of the faculty.

Sorry to bother you, but I don't have, uh, access to my phone, so I don't have Delia's number on me, and I can't remember the last few digits right — numbers aren't really my thing — and her aunt's unlisted, and I'd call her other aunt but that's sort of tricky, and then I found you in the Prescott directory — I only have last year's and Delia's not in it — anyhow, I was hoping you could give me her number. But you're not there. And you can't call me, because this isn't my phone and I'll need to put it back soon. And now I'm rambling. Sorry about that. But maybe you could give Delia a message, if it's not too much trouble? Would you mind telling her —

He paused, as if he was trying to figure out how to word his message. And then, in the background, there was a sudden creaking noise, like the hinges of a door opening, and a woman cried out.

The recording ended with an abrupt click, before Quinn could say what he wanted Natalie to tell me. But I guessed Fiona had found her cell phone.

Knowing that Quinn had been trying to reach me didn't solve any problems, but it did make me feel less like the world was coming to an end. Even if he was in serious trouble, I could put any concerns about him losing interest to temporary rest, and there was something totally endearing about how awkward he'd sounded. I spent most of my morning classes replaying his words in my head.

And then physics rolled around, leaving only the quiz standing between me and freedom. I tried to act surprised when Dr. Penske told us to put everything away except our pens and calculators, though he actually winked at me as he distributed the xeroxed copies. And as soon as I turned the paper over I saw Natalie had been right — the quiz was almost identical to her study guide, just without the Edward parts. I didn't even feel completely lost as I worked my way through the problems. Of course, Charley's dramatic reading had included tributes to the entire *90210* cast, so I kept hearing Luke Perry and Tori Spelling in my head as I tried to remember which steps to take.

Either way, when Dr. Penske called time, I was pretty sure I'd at least passed. And then it was like Charley was tracking our status remotely, because a hall monitor came in with a note for me to report to the office.

Except it turned out Charley had nothing to do with it. Mr. Seton had called me in there all on his own.

I arrived fully expecting to be told Charley would be picking me up for a forgotten doctor's appointment. And even when the receptionist said Mr. Seton wanted to see me personally, I only thought maybe he'd decided to use the occasion of my passing through his office for a quick headmaster-to-student chat.

But once I'd been ushered into his inner sanctum, he gestured for me to sit in one of the chairs opposite his desk, and then he sat down in his own chair, steepling his fingers beneath his chin.

"Miss Truesdale, as I'm sure you're aware, it has recently come to the attention of the administration that several members of our senior class have engaged in an inappropriate business venture, and, in doing so, abused Prescott's facilities and resources."

"Uh, yes, I heard about that," I said, confused.

"It also has not escaped our attention that you have become quite friendly with one of the seniors suspected of playing a pivotal role in these regrettable activities."

Mr. Seton obviously wasn't referring to Grey — he'd already been caught and confessed, so he wasn't "suspected." Besides, it was impossible to become "quite friendly" with somebody who seemed to be sleeping with his eyes open most of the time.

Which meant Mr. Seton was referring to Quinn, who was the only other senior I really knew apart from Gwyneth. But

128

since I still didn't understand what was happening, I only said, "Do you mean Quinn?"

"Correct. And I've asked you here to give you the opportunity to come forward of your own volition and share with me any knowledge of the inappropriate activities to which you were privy as a function of your relationship with Mr. Riley."

If I'd had my wits more about me, I might have asked how summoning me to his office constituted giving me the opportunity to come forward of my own volition, but I was too busy being baffled. "I wasn't privy to anything."

"You're certain of that?" he said, like he was certain of something very different.

"I'm certain."

"Completely certain?"

"Completely certain." And then, because I really couldn't figure out what was going on, I asked, "Did Quinn say I knew something?"

"No. Mr. Riley has been less than forthcoming on this matter. I was hoping you would be more cooperative."

And maybe because this had all come from so out of the blue and maybe because of the ridiculously large quantity of other things I was stressed about, I stopped being baffled and started being angry. In fact, I might have lost it. "So, Quinn hasn't told you anything, but you called me in here because you hoped I'd narc on him?"

"I don't believe 'narc' is the accurate term —"

129

"Is this what you did to him?"

"Excuse me?"

"Did you call him in here and say you were giving him the opportunity to come forward of his own volition and then when he wouldn't tell you anything you suspended him?"

"That's hardly a fair descrip —"

"Are you going to suspend me, too, for not telling you what I don't know?"

"Miss Truesdale, I have no interest in suspending you. Unless, of course, I discover that you have engaged in activities that merit suspension —"

"I haven't. And I don't know anything about what Quinn did or didn't do. How can I be privy when I never see Quinn or talk to Quinn or get so much as a complete message from Quinn?"

Mr. Seton didn't answer that. He just waited a moment, as if to make sure I really was done. Then he spoke. "Thank you, Miss Truesdale. That will be all for now. You may go."

Seventeen

Charley was waiting in the reception area, since when she'd called to get me out of class she'd been told I was already in Mr. Seton's office. And as soon as I explained what had happened, she wanted to march in there and tell him off herself, but I managed to convince her that would be overkill. Two Truesdale tantrums in one day might be more than Mr. Seton could handle, and I didn't want to give him any reason to get Patience involved. It seemed wisest to flee before it occurred to anyone to question Charley's excuse for taking me out of school. I mean, how many sixteen-year-olds actually needed to be rushed to emergency appointments with their herbalists?

Not that we were doing any such thing. In reality, Charley had arranged for us to meet Rafe nearby, at the oval-shaped boat pond in Central Park. The rain had stopped, but the weather was still misty and gray, so there wouldn't be too many people out — we'd be able to talk in relative privacy.

Rafe, however, had arrived at the boat pond before us, and he'd been unable to resist renting one of the radio-controlled miniature sloops from the concessions stand. He'd also challenged a bunch of little kids to a race, and he was crowing in victory when we showed up. Of course, then one of the kids started to cry, so he felt obligated to stage a rematch and let her win.

That done, he trotted over to join us at the table we'd found in the café area and gratefully accepted a cup of the hot chocolate we'd bought at the counter. And as he was working through his initial blushing and stammering in Charley's presence, we brought him up-to-date on everything we'd learned while he was gone.

By the time we'd finished, Rafe had restored himself to a functioning condition, and he addressed my most immediate fears first. "Your mother is quite safe," he said. "I assure you, there is no cause for concern. She is understandably frustrated by her inability to act more directly, but she recognizes the need for caution. In the meantime, she and Mark are well disguised and in comfortable accommodations, and they are taking the most stringent of measures to protect their welfare. And Mark is highly skilled in Krav Maga."

"What's Krav Maga?" I asked.

"It's a form of martial arts that draws from both boxing and wrestling," Rafe explained. "It originated in Bratislava in the nineteen thirties but is now widely deployed among elite military units around the globe. Mark became proficient when he trained with the Israeli Defense Forces."

"What kind of climate change specialist trains with the Israeli Defense Forces?" asked Charley.

"Mark is not your typical climate change specialist," said Rafe. "You'll enjoy meeting him."

Given T.K.'s situation, I was glad Mark knew martial arts, but I was less interested in meeting him than in figuring out what we were going to do to get him and my mother back to their respective homes. "Did you find out about the people from the *Polar Star*?" I asked.

Rafe removed his glasses and wiped them on his tie. Today it was spotted leopards on a navy background. "When I landed in Buenos Aires, I checked in with your mother, to make sure she was well and to apprise her of your own status and our investigation. She concurred that the *Polar Star* was a logical starting point, and she was able to provide me with the name of the captain she'd originally hired, an Alejandro Frers. I then took another flight to Tierra del Fuego, as this man lived in Ushuaia, the primary port in the region."

"And did you find him?" asked Charley.

Rafe put his glasses back on. "I assumed this would be a simple task, as Ushuaia is quite small — a town rather than a city. Yet Frers is a common name in the area, especially among the seafaring classes. When I ultimately arrived at the correct address, his landlady said he had moved out in August, leaving no forwarding information. Nor were the local authorities able to provide further details."

"Oh," I said, not sure what to make of that. "Then it was a dead end?"

Rafe held up a finger in gentle admonishment. "I did not give up so easily, Delia. I spent that night and the next in every drinking establishment along the docks. I am still feeling the effects of those two nights, but it was not without purpose. I struck up a number of conversations with men who work on the ships sailing in and out of the port. Most of these conversations were fruitless, but eventually I found a man who could help."

"Did he know how to find Alejandro Frers?"

"He didn't, no. But he told me a curious story."

Apparently, the guy Rafe met at the bar knew somebody who knew somebody who knew one of the original crew members on the *Polar Star*, so the story he told Rafe was more hearsay than any of Gwyneth's information about Edward. But it fit in so well with everything else, it seemed like it had to be true. Even better, it ended up giving me a way to act on Carolina's dream without having to explain I'd been speaking to Carolina.

The reason Alejandro Frers was nowhere to be found was that he'd hightailed it out of town, shortly after a mysterious brown-haired woman showed up and exchanged an enormous sum of money for the title to the *Polar Star* and his guarantee that he'd disappear for good.

"That sort of thing really happens?" Charley asked, like she hadn't been paying attention to all of the other crazy things that had occurred in the last six weeks. "People just agree to disappear?"

"Was it the same brown-haired woman I saw here in New York?" I said. "It had to be, right?"

"Your description and the description of the woman in Ushuaia were uncannily similar," said Rafe. "It would be a tremendous coincidence to find two individual women matching the same description playing a role in this plot. I am inclined to believe they are one and the same. The man I met called her 'La Morena.'"

I wondered how much of a coincidence Rafe would think it was if he knew Carolina called her the same thing.

"Her trench coat must have deep pockets," said Charley. "Buying an entire ship and convincing someone to leave his entire life behind can't come cheap."

"And the deep pockets support the entire EAROFO theory," I added. "A group of oil companies wouldn't have a hard time coming up with that much cash."

"Delia, I hope you remember what I said about shooting the messenger, but neither would Hunter Riley," said Charley.

"I know, but while we have no idea what Hunter's up to, and it probably is bad since he lied to his family and everyone in his office, we still haven't heard about him hanging out with a brown-haired woman, and we know for a fact that she was in Navitaco's offices." Then I added, not even trying to be subtle, "It sounds like she's more important than we realized. Maybe we should be trying to locate her, too."

135

"I agree," said Rafe. "If this woman is paying people off, odds are that she's created an electronic trail — records of bank withdrawals and wire transfers and the like. And this trail is precisely the type of evidence we require. If we can connect Alejandro Frers to La Morena and La Morena to the source of the money, whether it's EAROFO or Hunter Riley or someone else altogether, we'll have what we need."

"So how can we do that?" asked Charley. "Do we have any chance of ever finding Alejandro Frers?"

"Possibly. There are a few leads I will follow when I return to South America. And the reason I came back to New York was to talk to a colleague who is skilled in investigating financial records. But it would be useful to try to identify La Morena in parallel. Perhaps she is employed directly by one of the EAROFO member companies?"

"Not Navitaco," I said. "That's one thing I know for sure. And not by Hunter Riley, either." While I'd been waiting for the sun to rise that morning, I'd done my best to remember every single detail of our five encounters, hoping I'd think of something that would help us locate this anonymous woman. But the best I'd come up with was less of a lead than an antilead. Now I explained.

"At the office building where Navitaco and Hunter Riley both have their offices, I had to sign in as a visitor on the ground floor, and they gave me a pass for security. There was a specific entrance and exit for visitors, and on the way in, you had to

136

swipe your pass, and on the way out, you had to return it to the guard. And when I saw her that day, leaving Navitaco's offices, La Morena went through the visitors' gate and turned in a visitors' pass."

Rafe and Charley both looked impressed by my powers of deduction, though they just as quickly reached the same conclusion I had, that this specific deduction didn't bring us any closer to identifying the woman.

And then it came to me.

"They made me sign in," I said.

"What?" said Charley.

"When I was a visitor, to the office building. They made me sign in and show my ID, and they had my name on a list of people they were expecting. So, if La Morena was a visitor —"

"Then she also would have appeared on the visitors' list," said Rafe, finishing my thought.

"So we need to get our hands on the list," said Charley, catching on. "But how can we do that?"

I knew exactly how we could do it.

Or, more accurately, I knew someone who might be able to do it for us.

Eighteen

I was worried Natalie would be so busy either moping over Edward or figuring out how to try him before a jury of his peers that she wouldn't be interested in some friendly hacking. But she responded to my text right when school ended, like she was eager for the distraction. She was doing a research internship at Columbia and had to go there for a couple of hours first, but she promised she'd head for the loft as soon as she was done.

True to her word, she arrived at Laight Street a little after six. And in typical Natalie fashion, she'd stopped home to pick up some computer equipment she knew I'd never have, but she hadn't bothered to change out of her Prescott uniform. I could tell Charley was already planning where we'd take her shopping to thank her for what she was about to do, though Charley had no idea what she'd be up against — Natalie would probably wear Garanimals if they came in her size, so she wouldn't have to waste valuable time trying to match outfits herself.

"It was the weirdest thing," said Natalie as she walked in. "I took a taxi here, and the inside was covered in stickers with pictures of the two of you. There were seventeen on the partition between the driver and the backseat, three on one door, four on the other door, and seven on the rear window. Why would somebody paste thirty-one stickers with your pictures on them in the back of a taxi?"

"Stickers," said Charley, resigned. "I should have seen that coming."

"What should you have seen coming?" asked Rafe from the kitchen. He was booked on an overnight flight back to Buenos Aires, but he was hanging out with us until it was time to leave for the airport. He said it was to help Natalie, but since Natalie was an accomplished hacker and Rafe still hadn't mastered the lock on his briefcase, it was pretty obvious he was just trying to squeeze in every possible moment he could with Charley. He'd even offered to cook dinner. Now he was rummaging through the refrigerator for ingredients, though we'd warned him all he'd find was leftover takeout.

Anyhow, Charley began telling Rafe about Dieter harnessing the power of visual media, and Natalie and I got to work. Which really meant that I brought out my laptop so Natalie could work on both of our computers at once while I tried not to get in her way.

It didn't take long for me to explain to Natalie what we were trying to accomplish and why. "What's the address of the office building?" she asked, her fingers poised over one of the keyboards. "First we need to determine who handles security for the property."

I gave her the building's address on West 40th Street, across from Bryant Park and the main branch of the New York Public Library, and from there it only took her a couple of Web searches to identify the firm that managed the property and then the vendor the firm used for security.

"Perfect," she said, pulling up the vendor's site and giving it a quick scan. "They have an intranet so their clients can log in remotely and access their records. Once I've accessed the intranet, I should be able to get exactly what you need."

It seemed like breaching the security of a security firm should be extra challenging, but the prospect didn't faze Natalie at all. She almost seemed disappointed that her mission was so straightforward.

"Great," I said. "What should I do to help?"

"I'd love a glass of water," Natalie said, which was her way of telling me to leave her alone. She was already rummaging in her bag, pulling out an assortment of complicated-looking gadgets and wiring our laptops together to construct a makeshift high-speed data processor. So I got her a glass of water and went to join Charley and Rafe over at the kitchen end of the loft.

Charley was sitting on one of the stools at the counter, keeping Rafe company as he sorted through the items he'd unearthed in the refrigerator. His pleasant expression was strained, as if he was trying not to show how horrified he was by what he was learning about our eating habits.

"I can't believe we didn't think of this before," Charley said to me when I climbed up on the stool next to her.

"Think of what?" I asked. "Getting Rafe to clean out the refrigerator?"

"No, though it is very sweet of him. I was talking about getting him to help us find Dieter. He had the most fabulous idea."

The combination of the "sweet" and the "fabulous idea" made Rafe start blushing and stammering all over again. "It was only a suggestion," he managed to say. "And perhaps not a practical one."

"I think it's brilliant," said Charley. "It would never have occurred to me to reach out to the Department of Homeland Security."

Putting Dieter on a terrorist watch list seemed like an extreme solution to an only somewhat extreme problem, but Charley was happy, and that was all Rafe cared about.

Maybe twenty minutes later, as Rafe was insisting he could make a casserole from leftover schnitzel and kung pao chicken if only he had some ketchup, and Charley and I were suggesting we might be better off ordering in from the taco place, Natalie called out. "Delia, I think you'll want to see this."

I rushed over to where she was working at the big table in the middle of the room. "Did you get access to the intranet?"

"No, not yet. But this just popped up on your computer," she

141

said, turning one of the laptops toward me so I could see the instant message on the screen.

OLIVICE: yt?

The cursor blinked impatiently, waiting for my reply. "Who's Olivice?" asked Natalie.

"Yes, Delia. Do you know this Olivice?" asked Rafe. He and Charley had followed me over, and now the four of us were huddled in front of the screen.

"No. But it can't hurt to write back, can it?" I said.

None of us could think of a reason why I shouldn't, so I typed in a wary response.

DELIATRUE: ?

The answer came practically before I'd hit return.

OLIVICE: Quinn
OLIVICE: Oliver + Beatrice = Olivice
OLIVICE: playroom PC

Charley made a triumphant noise behind me. "I told you so," she said.

"Told her what?" asked Rafe.

"Delia decided Quinn was losing interest in her, and I told her that was insane because it's obvious he's into her, and then we found out he was in trouble at school, but Delia decided that might make him unworthy, which was ridiculous because she has no idea what's truly going on and we all know she still likes him anyway, and then she hasn't been able to talk to him because his stepmother won't let him talk to anyone, but he tried to call her last night, which he wouldn't have done if he didn't like her, and now here he is, getting in touch with her again, which just goes to show I was right all along."

"Quinn's in trouble at school?" said Rafe, seizing upon one of the few facts buried in Charley's torrent of words. "Is this a suitable companion for Delia? A young man with disciplinary problems might be a bad influence, and Delia is at a very formative age."

"I don't think Quinn's a bad influence. There is the issue with his father, but as I know all too well, one can't choose one's own relations, otherwise I would have gotten rid of Patty a long time ago —"

"May I have some privacy, please?" I demanded.

And, thankfully, Charley and Rafe returned to the kitchen, taking Natalie with them to help arbitrate the casserole-versus-tacos dispute.

Meanwhile, as I turned back to the screen I felt the uncontrollable smile spreading over my face yet again. Not that I was sure what to write back — I had so many questions for Quinn at this point, I didn't know where to start.

DELIATRUE: what's going on?
OLIVICE: too complicated
OLIVICE: no time now
OLIVICE: meet me tmrw?

Charley would be proud of the way I threw caution to the wind.

DELIATRUE: where/when?
OLIVICE: 3? nat hist mus?
DELIATRUE: c u then

And that was it. Or so I thought. Because I was about to sign off when Olivice popped up again.

OLIVICE: miss u, juliet

And then that really was it.

But the uncontrollable smile stayed on my face for the rest of the night.

Nineteen

It wasn't easy, but we eventually managed to convince Rafe that a kung pao–schnitzel casserole sounded delicious but might not be what we were in the mood for that particular night. Then Charley phoned in our taco order, the two of them went to pick it up, and we all had dinner together.

Rafe left for the airport soon after, and Natalie returned to hacking the security firm's intranet while Charley and I pretended to keep ourselves busy. Around ten, though, Natalie pushed her chair away from the table in frustration. "I'm in," she announced. "But there's a problem."

She'd been able to access the intranet, but the information we wanted was shielded behind an additional wall of security. "They're asking for a scan of the barcode on an approved individual's ID card," Natalie explained. "I can run a program that will try randomly generated barcodes, but there's a virtually infinite number of permutations, so it could take days and maybe even weeks to hit on one that will work, and the longer the program runs, the greater the risk it will trigger an alert that the intranet's been compromised. Is there any way to get our hands on the ID card of a building tenant?"

We all knew exactly how we could accomplish precisely that, but we also knew just how loaded such a course of action would be.

Because hacking into a Web site was one thing — we needed to find La Morena for reasons of self-defense and climate preservation, and Natalie was too skilled to bring the site crashing down or to otherwise leave tracks.

But asking Quinn to go rooting through his father's belongings so we could borrow an ID card might be crossing an ethical line. It only complicated matters further that I was still under strict instructions not to discuss the investigation with him — even if I was comfortable asking him for Hunter's ID, I'd be skating dangerously near the topic of what we were trying to accomplish and why, and from there it was only a short step to his father's potential role in the whole scenario.

So we were at a temporary impasse, since our next best idea was to find out what other companies were in the building and make an appointment with one of them in order to obtain another visitor's pass. And while this would probably work, it would also have to wait until business hours resumed on Monday, which meant our chances of solving this problem over the weekend were pretty much shot.

Natalie was disappointed, but Charley and I appreciated that she'd gotten as far as she had, and Natalie actually seemed sincere when she said she'd had a good time. "As soon as I get home, I'll start the program to try the randomly generated barcodes.

146

It's not mathematically impossible that we'll arrive at a match quickly, before we need to worry about raising any red flags on their end."

She gathered up her things, and we accompanied her downstairs. It was getting late, so we wanted to see her safely into a taxi, and we also had to replenish our ice cream supply at the twenty-four-hour deli.

As the elevator made its slow descent, Charley turned to Natalie. "I hope you have something fun planned for the rest of the weekend."

To the casual observer, this would appear to be perfectly innocent small talk, but I knew better. Charley was fishing for an opportunity to give Natalie her two cents about Edward — it wouldn't surprise me if she thought she really did have a shot at the Presidential Medal of Freedom. Earlier, when Charley and Rafe were busy in the kitchen, I'd asked Natalie myself what she'd decided to do, and she'd said she still wasn't sure. Either way, I wasn't surprised when she opened up to Charley now, telling her the whole story. Everybody opened up to Charley.

"I'm supposed to go out with this guy tomorrow night, but I've learned some disturbing information about his past," Natalie confided. "There are significant discrepancies between how he presents himself to me and his broader reputation."

"Do you like how he presents himself to you?" asked Charley.

147

"Well, yes," said Natalie, and that was all it took for her to start gushing to Charley the same way she'd gushed to me. She kept it up as we made our way across Laight Street and over to Hudson Street, where we'd be able to hail a taxi to take her uptown.

But when we reached the corner, she stopped short and told Charley what Gwyneth had said. "I just don't know how to weigh the data points from my personal experience against the third-party data points," she concluded.

"Is it possible you're overthinking this?" said Charley.

Overthinking was an unfamiliar concept to Natalie. "What do you mean?"

"Obviously, you want to make sure the guy isn't an ax murderer or anything. But shouldn't how Edward is with you be the most important data point of all?"

It sounded so simple when Charley said it, but I had the feeling Natalie would be debating it with herself the entire way home.

The next day, Charley and I spent the whole morning and a good chunk of the early afternoon figuring out what I'd wear to meet Quinn at the Museum of Natural History. This would have been hard enough under normal circumstances, but not knowing what the afternoon held in store made it that much more problematic.

So left to my own devices, getting dressed probably would've taken a while. But with Charley involved it sucked up every available second, starting almost at dawn and continuing until we were dangerously close to being late.

After I'd tried on everything in my closet and most of the items in Charley's, we ultimately agreed on a cream-colored Marc Jacobs dress with a scoop neck and black banding at the waist, topped off by a cropped lavender jacket and, in honor of my destination, the cuff with the elephant we'd bought at Barney's.

Charley took a step back to better appreciate her work, her brow furrowed in thought. "It's good, almost perfect, but something's missing, and I can't quite put my finger on what —" Then she interrupted herself. "Wait here," she ordered, dashing out of my room.

She returned brandishing a black fedora with braided trim. "Here you go."

"I don't know if I'm a hat sort of person," I said, though I knew from experience this was just begging for a discourse on how I absolutely was a hat person but hadn't yet been exposed to the right hat and fortune was smiling on me today because the hat she had in her hand would change my mind forever.

"There's only one way to find out," said Charley, setting the fedora on my head.

But it turned out I have a very small skull, which might also explain why I had so little room for processing certain types of physics-related information. The fedora slipped down so low over my face even Charley couldn't argue it was wearable if I actually wanted to see. "Well," she said, disappointed. "We'll just have to do more shopping."

More shopping wasn't going to happen anytime soon, though, since it was already half past two. And given what we'd heard about La Morena making people disappear, Charley definitely wasn't letting me go anywhere unescorted — we ended up running for the subway together. But as luck would have it, we caught an express train and reached the museum with a few minutes to spare.

Charley waited with me out front, by the statue of Teddy Roosevelt mounted on a horse, surveying the traffic on Central Park West. As all the parents with their little kids and tourists with cameras streamed by, she detailed the fabulous places we'd shop for hats once I'd embraced the vital importance of hats as a wardrobe staple.

I had to admit, I was glad Charley didn't need me to hold up my end of the conversation. I'd been able to keep it together while we'd been planning my outfit, but now that we were actually there, with Quinn due to arrive at any second, I couldn't ignore the overwhelming sense that a pivotal, do-or-die moment was approaching, the sort of moment when things were decided in a completely irreversible way.

So as we waited, each second felt like an hour, and the people going in and out of the museum seemed to move in slow motion. And just when I was beginning to wonder if I'd messed up, if

Quinn's IM hadn't said three o'clock but an entirely different time and maybe even a different place, a cab pulled up and he got out.

He wasn't alone, of course — Bea and Oliver spilled onto the sidewalk after him. Charley and I had been expecting they'd come along, since otherwise the museum as a destination was sort of random. Volunteering to take the two of them here was probably the only way Quinn had been able to convince Fiona to let him leave the house.

"Just as we thought," observed Charley. "Using the kids as a get-out-of-jail-free card."

I couldn't respond. I hadn't seen Quinn in more than seventy-two hours, and the sight of him induced full-on brain paralysis.

The day was cool and damp again, but Quinn was like a magnet for what little sun there was. A single ray escaped from behind the clouds, and the light turned his sand-colored hair to gold. Then his eyes landed on me, and the drab autumn day suddenly felt like summer.

By the time I recovered, Charley had said hello and good-bye and conveniently disappeared, Oliver had greeted me with his standard fist bump, and Bea had given me a big hug and was chattering excitedly about dinosaurs and butterflies.

"This way, guys," said Quinn, putting one hand on Bea's head and the other on Oliver's and pointing them in the direction of the museum entrance. "March."

As soon as they were moving forward, Quinn turned to me. "Hey," he said.

"Hey," I said back. The uncontrollable smile was spreading across my face, and there wasn't a thing I could do about it.

But it didn't seem to matter, because a similar smile was on his face.

Then he was drawing me to him, and I felt the heat of his lips against mine.

Twenty

I could have stayed in that spot for the rest of my life. Nothing could compete with how completely right it felt to be there with Quinn, standing by the Teddy Roosevelt statue and kissing.

But reality intruded in the form of what sounded like a mob of people laughing and clapping. When we pulled apart, I saw we'd attracted a small crowd of spectators and some of them were even taking our picture. I probably should've been mortified, but I was too giddy from the kissing.

Meanwhile, Bea and Oliver had figured out we weren't directly behind them and come back to retrieve us. "Dude, you're embarrassing me," Oliver muttered to Quinn as Bea grabbed my hand and began towing me toward the museum entrance.

Quinn had promised them we'd go see the model whale, and I guessed this was an old favorite because they led the way through the thronged lobby and to the Hall of Ocean Life like homing pigeons. Once there, they wanted to give me a guided tour, but Quinn offered up pizza for dinner and Bea a piggyback ride on the trip home in return for time to ourselves. And after negotiating pepperoni versus sausage and what duration of piggyback ride Bea could expect, they reached an agreement.

So Bea and Oliver wandered off to explore, and Quinn and I found a bench in the upper gallery, almost parallel with the massive whale suspended from the ceiling and with a clear view of the hall so we could keep an eye on the kids. And though I knew we had a lot to cover and the clock was ticking — Quinn's get-out-of-jail-free card had to expire at some point — when he moved closer to me on the bench, it was impossible not to start kissing again.

"Nice," he said.

That seemed like an understatement. "Really nice," I said.

And then we kissed some more.

"Well," Quinn said when we next came up for air. "You're probably wondering what's been happening."

That was also an understatement. At least, that's what I would've thought if all of the kissing hadn't pretty much erased my ability to think. "A bit," I admitted.

"I tried to call you — Oliver had buried Fiona's cell phone under a sofa cushion when she wasn't looking — but you probably already know how that backfired."

"Was Fiona angry?" I asked.

"Angrier, you mean? I don't think that's even possible."

"So, what is going on?"

The light in the room had a dim, underwater feel, and in its bluish tint Quinn's eyes looked more gray than green. I wondered whether the way they changed color from moment to moment had more to do with the light or what was going on in his head. Now he seemed to be ordering his thoughts, like he was trying to decide where to start. "Okay," he said, taking a deep breath. "I should get this part out of the way. I didn't do it. The gambling thing. I wasn't involved."

I registered a vague sense of relief.

Until he added, "But it was my idea. I thought it up over the summer."

"You what?"

"You know how my dad wants me to go to the finance program at Wharton?"

I nodded. "He went there, too, right?"

"Right. But with my math grades, it's going to be a long shot. So I was trying to come up with ideas for businesses I could start, to show I at least have potential. And the poker thing was one of my ideas. Not the part about targeting underage kids or hosting it at Prescott — that was moronic — just the basic concept. But I realized that even if I could get the right licenses and figure out the logistics, an admissions officer might not look so favorably on gambling as an extracurricular activity. When school started up again, I forgot about the whole thing, but I also forgot I'd told some of the guys. They ran with it on their own."

"Then why didn't you just say so to Mr. Seton?" I asked. "You shouldn't get in trouble for something you didn't do."

He'd been holding one of my hands, but now he let it slip from his grasp. "It's not that easy," he said.

"Why not?" It seemed pretty cut-and-dried to me, and I also wanted him to take my hand back.

"Because Seton would want to know who I told, so he can go after them all. He says it's a matter of principle."

"Oh," I said, starting to understand. And after my own conversation with the headmaster, I knew exactly what Quinn was up against — Mr. Seton had very different views on what was and wasn't principled behavior than the average high school student. "It seems like it's a lot more honorable not to start naming names."

"I know. But he keeps asking for details, and he's threatening to expel me if I don't talk, and somehow the whole thing . . ." His voice trailed off.

"What?" I asked.

"It just brings up bad memories."

I thought I knew which bad memories he was talking about. Part of the custody battle Quinn's parents had involved him testifying against his own mother. And while that had been years ago, I could see how Mr. Seton pressuring him to turn on his friends would dredge it all up again.

"I'm sorry," I said, though the words seemed inadequate.

Quinn shrugged. "The irony is that there I was, trying to figure out how to get myself into Wharton, and it's going to result in my not getting in anywhere because I'm going to be thrown out of Prescott. And the bigger irony is that it won't even matter, because once Hunter finds out, he's going to kill me, so neither of us will have to worry about my future."

"There you go," I said. "You found the silver lining." Which wasn't funny, but we both started to laugh anyway.

And after that we had to kiss some more.

When we paused again, a few minutes later, Quinn said, "Sorry to bore you. I know you have more important things to worry about."

"This is important, and I'm not bored," I said. In fact, I was happier than I'd been in a long time. I mean, I recognized Quinn was in a difficult position, and I didn't have the slightest clue as to how he could extract himself. But from a purely selfish perspective, it was a huge weight off my shoulders to confirm he wasn't in fact a moron, and based on the way he'd been kissing me all afternoon, it also seemed safe to conclude that he hadn't lost interest in me.

"It's going to seem boring after you hear the other thing I have to tell you," he said.

"What other thing?" I asked, feeling a twinge of apprehension.

He shifted his weight on the bench and turned to sit facing me rather than side by side, the way we'd been before. And when I saw his expression, the twinge blossomed into something much larger.

"I know I should have told you this part first," Quinn said.

"But then, right when I saw you, I didn't want to ruin it, and after that I figured you must have been wondering about what's been happening at school, too, so I thought I might as well get that cleared up, though the reality was I was only putting off telling you the other thing I need to tell you because it's a lot harder to explain, and it's also going to sound crazy, and it's not like I'm sure about any of it, so it's tempting not to talk about it, especially since there's a good chance you're going to hate me when I tell you."

"Tell me what already?" I said. Not only was he starting to make Charley seem succinct, he was making me seriously nervous. What could he possibly say that would make me hate him? Was I about to be treated to some details about Quinn that would make Edward Vargas look like one of Dr. Penske's Cub Scouts?

But that wasn't it at all.

He took another deep breath and exhaled slowly. "It's my dad. I think he's involved in what happened to your mother."

Twenty-one

"What?" I managed to say.

"I know, it's hard to believe," said Quinn.

Of course, Quinn had no way of knowing just how easy it was for me to believe, but that didn't mean I expected to hear him voicing the same suspicions. And that he had suspicions at all seemed to confirm we'd been right to have them.

A chill went through me, followed by an ugly sense of resignation. It looked as though our kissing would be forever tainted in my memory by this conversation coming so quickly on its heels.

Because now not only would I have to act like I hadn't had my own concerns about Hunter — I mean, it was one thing to decide your own parent's an evildoer, but it was an entirely different thing for the person you were just kissing to tell you she'd thought so, too — I also had a responsibility to pump Quinn for any new information he could offer. And that seemed both unavoidable and wrong in every way.

"This trip Hunter's on in Argentina — it doesn't fit," Quinn was saying. "Nobody at his office knew, so it can't be a normal business thing. Meanwhile, Fiona's freaking out because she

159

thinks he's having an affair, but I don't think that's it, either. Hunter really loves her, and he'd never do anything that would hurt the kids. But he's definitely in Argentina. He was on the phone the night before he left, setting up a meeting, and I heard him specifically say Buenos Aires and even the name of his hotel there, and he had his professional voice on — he didn't sound like he was romancing anyone. But it didn't have to do with his regular work."

"Isn't it sort of a leap from having mysterious meetings in Buenos Aires to being in on the whole conspiracy?" I asked, hoping I didn't sound as awkward as I felt.

"That was just the beginning. When everything broke at school, Fiona grounded me, which for her means I'm not even allowed to talk to anyone. She took my laptop and cell phone, and she kept hitting redial on the house phone to check I wasn't making calls out. But Thursday, while she was picking the kids up from school, I tried the PC in my dad's home office. I know his log-in information — he's got a thing for James Bond, and double-O seven works every time — so booting up wasn't a problem. But even though Fiona thinks Argentina's in Mexico, she's strangely tech savvy. She'd changed the password on our Wi-Fi network — I couldn't get online. But I did find a file named 'Ross' on the hard drive."

Along with the ugly resignation and awkwardness, I now felt a sense of déjà vu. It had been only a couple of weeks since I'd found the folder labeled Ross among my mother's papers, with a copy of her correspondence with EAROFO and a geologic map of the Ross Sea inside. "The same Ross?"

He nodded. "It was a chart showing the potential oil output from the Ross Sea given different rates of production and also how the profits — hundreds of millions of dollars — would be split among a bunch of different players. Navitaco was on there, along with Perkins Oil and Energex and all of the other EAROFO companies."

Another chill went through me. The chart he was describing was like our theory translated into cold, hard numbers; its very existence transformed pure speculation to concrete fact.

My next question was the most difficult one so far, but I knew I had to ask. "Was your dad's name on the chart, too?"

"No," said Quinn. "But it doesn't matter — that's not how he operates. He'll make his money from having inside knowledge of the output levels. And if you're thinking maybe this isn't what it looks like, and it doesn't mean he's in on the entire thing — trust me, when you're grounded and you can't talk to anyone but your infuriated stepmother, a six-year-old girl, an eight-year-old boy, their nanny, and the housekeeper, you have a lot of time to examine the facts from every angle and try to come up with other explanations for how they fit together. But I kept coming back to this: Why would Hunter have that spreadsheet if he's not part of it?"

Quinn was right — it was pretty damning.

We were both quiet for a while, each thinking our separate thoughts. Quinn was staring down at the hall below, but I doubted he really saw anything just then except that spreadsheet with all of its incriminating information. And I only wished there was something I could say or do to make him feel better. I mean, the mess at Prescott was bad enough. Stumbling onto his father's involvement in a plot that at best was limited to environmental destruction and at worst included attempted murder must have been devastating.

"So now that I've told you, do you?" Quinn said suddenly, breaking the silence.

"Do I what?" I asked.

He brought his gaze up to meet mine. "Hate me."

That thought was too foreign to possibly answer with words. So I kissed him instead.

In the spirit of looking for the silver lining, there no longer seemed to be any reason not to bring Quinn fully up-to-date on the investigation, though I carefully excised the part about us suspecting his father all along. And another silver lining was that Quinn was able to solve one of our immediate problems. He'd spent part of his summer interning in his father's office, and he still had an active security pass for the building, complete with the barcode, right there in his wallet.

He dug it out and handed it over. "It's the least I can do," he said with a small, unhappy laugh. "In fact, at this point it's the only thing I can do. I don't think I've ever felt so useless in my life."

"This is a huge help," I tried to assure him. "Now we can find La Morena."

He glanced at his watch. "You'd have found her anyway. But if I don't get the kids home soon, Fiona will probably end up grounding them, too. She's on a real rampage."

So he took my hand and we went to find Bea and Oliver.

"Dude, I'm starving, and you said we'd order pizza," said Oliver when we located them at the sea otter diorama.

"Is Delia coming home with us for dinner?" asked Bea.

"Quinn's grounded," said Oliver. "Grounded people can't have friends over. And remember, you can't say anything about Delia meeting us here or Quinn will get in even more trouble."

"What's more trouble than being grounded?" said Bea.

"I don't think we want to find out," said Quinn.

Quinn hailed a cab for me out on Central Park West, in front of the museum. It was weird saying good-bye when neither of us knew how we were next going to be in touch. The nanny leaving the playroom PC online and unattended had been a fluke, and it wasn't likely that Fiona would restore Quinn's phone and computer privileges anytime soon. She was definitely going to be a lot more careful about the whereabouts of her own phone.

So when he kissed me one final time, the kiss felt less giddy and more serious, like it would have to sustain us for a while.

But in spite of everything, it had the same impact. The world around me went fuzzy, and by the time it solidified again I was in the taxi and heading downtown.

Twenty-two

The rest of the evening was totally anticlimactic. At least, most of it was.

I borrowed Charley's scanner and sent an image of Quinn's ID card to Natalie, but she was busy doing whatever it was she'd decided to do with Edward and I knew she wouldn't get to it until the next day. Meanwhile, Charley didn't believe in going out on Saturday nights ("too dull, with the boring married couples having date night"), so we ordered in pizza, because Charley felt that way I could dine with Quinn in spirit, and we also watched *Say Anything* as we ate, because Charley said it offered striking parallels with my current situation.

"How?" I said. "The Ione Skye character's father cheated on his taxes. He didn't try to have the John Cusack character's mother killed."

"You're missing the point, which is love conquers all, even the felonious indiscretions of one's parents," said Charley. And then she shushed me, because John Cusack was standing outside Ione Skye's window, playing "In Your Eyes" on an old-fashioned boom box.

Anyhow, John Cusack and Ione Skye were flying off to

England and the credits were starting to roll when someone buzzed from downstairs.

"Are you expecting a visitor?" asked Charley.

"No, are you?"

"Not unless someone's cleverly designed an ice cream delivery service that anticipates one's needs before one has them," she said, going over to the intercom. "Hello?"

It turned out that the person downstairs did, in fact, have a relationship with mobile ice cream vendors. "Oh, yes, hello. It is I. Zere is ze party in ze flat above mine — I cannot sleep, and ze sleeplessness is very bad for my art. But I no longer have ze key. Vill you ring me in, please?"

It took a strange blend of oblivious confidence for Dieter to present himself at our door like that. Even Charley was at a momentary loss for words, which was saying a lot.

But she buzzed him in anyway, and as we listened to the elevator creaking up from the ground floor, she turned to me. "When I give the signal, you create a distraction and I'll hit him from behind."

I didn't think she was really serious, but I couldn't help but notice the way she was scanning the room for blunt objects.

"I hope you're proud of yourself," Charley said to Dieter as the elevator doors slid open.

It was pouring out, and Dieter looked like a drowned hamster. He'd remembered his scarf, but I guessed he'd forgotten his

166

umbrella. "Vat do you mean?" he asked. He seemed genuinely confused.

"What do I mean?" said Charley, incredulous. And then she exploded. "WHAT DO I MEAN?"

Dieter took a step backward. I did, too. Charley wasn't scary often, which made it extra scary when she was.

"Have you listened to none of my messages?" she demanded.

"Ze voice mail, it is for ze corporate drone. Not ze *cineaste*," he said.

"Well, Mr. Cineaste, you've turned our lives into an episode of *America's Most Wanted*, except the wrong way around since we're the good guys," she said. "And I couldn't care less about myself, but Delia has been entrusted, however unwisely, to my care by her mother, and I am responsible for her well-being. Somebody's already tried to kill her once on my watch. Why didn't you just put up maps showing the route here or promise a reward for whoever offs her first?"

"A map vould not achieve ze desired aesthetic effect, and a revard is so overtly commercial," said Dieter, wounded. "My concept is far superior."

"Your concept? What concept?" asked Charley.

Dieter drew himself up to his full height. "It is ze brilliant cultural experiment. I have harnessed ze power of visual media to mobilize ze power of ze masses, transforming ze entire city

167

into Delia's bodyguard. How can she come to harm ven everyvone looks after her?"

He actually had a point, in his own convoluted way.

I thought about what Carolina had said, about the posters being yellow — the color of caution. It made a lot more sense now.

And I had to admit, I sort of liked the idea of eight million people standing guard.

It was good to get that straightened out, though I was pretty sure the loft would no longer be Dieter's go-to place for peace and quiet. And that was Saturday night, and Sunday it was like the sun never came up, the weather was so gloomy and wet.

The morning dragged by, and then Charley tried to convince me to join her for lunch and a gallery show with a friend, but I was too distracted. Instead, I stayed at the loft, eating leftover pizza and waiting for Natalie to call. I was hoping she'd be able to crack open the security firm's intranet sooner rather than later so I could figure out my next move — I knew exactly how Quinn felt when he'd talked about feeling useless.

A little before three P.M., my phone finally rang and I snatched it up. "Natalie?"

"No," said a girl, and though the voice wasn't distinctive, I knew exactly who it was from the way she stretched the single syllable into a languorous four or five.

"Oh," I said, trying to hide my disappointment. "Hi, Gwyneth. How are you?"

"Fine."

This was followed by a long silence. In the background, a male narrator was describing the mating rituals of the black-footed ferret, and I could picture my cousin staring at the TV, her mouth slightly open and her eyes slightly glazed.

"Are you having a nice weekend?" I said eventually, speaking extra loudly in case Gwyneth had forgotten about me and no longer had the phone against her ear.

But she was still there. "Uh-huh," she said.

And then there was another long silence. I'd thought conversation with Gwyneth was challenging in person — trying to talk to her on the phone was like an extreme sport, but only in terms of the degree of difficulty and not because of any adrenaline rush.

"Well, thanks for calling," I finally said. "I guess I'll see you in school tomorrow."

"Okay," she said. And she hung up.

So that was a false alarm. But when the phone rang again, a half hour later, I was positive that this time it really would be Natalie and she'd have La Morena's identity all figured out.

"Natalie?" I said.

"No."

"Oh. Hi, Gwyneth. What's up?"

"Nothing," she said.

169

There was yet another long silence. But just as I was gearing up to get off the phone again, she spoke. "Quinn's missing."

"What do you mean, 'Quinn's missing'?"

"Fiona Riley just called my mom. Quinn disappeared between dinner last night and brunch this morning."

I probably should have been more surprised, but on some subconscious level I must have been expecting this. I mean, I'd seen the state he was in the previous day — it was pretty obvious Fiona's communications ban and everything else about being grounded was starting to wear on him. And if Quinn was gone, I also knew it had to be on purpose. People weren't abducted from buildings like his — nobody could make it up to the penthouse without first conquering an army of doormen and elevator attendants.

No, Quinn had clearly escaped. Now I was only wondering where he was — I would've hoped he'd come straight to me, but it sounded like he'd been on the lam for several hours at least, and I hadn't heard from him.

"Did he leave a note or anything?" I asked.

But I was talking to a dead phone. Gwyneth had already hung up.

I started dialing her number to call her back, but before I'd even hit SEND somebody buzzed the door from the street. I dropped the phone and dashed over to the intercom.

I pushed the button for the speaker. "Quinn?"

170

"No, it is not the Romeo. Now, why are you not unlocking the door? It is raining, and my shoes will be *destruido*."

I buzzed Carolina in.

"*Ay, dios!*" she cried as she stepped into the loft. "The rain, it does not stop."

She was dressed in a pale pink Hello Kitty rain slicker, complete with a matching Hello Kitty rain hat and umbrella.

"Can I get you anything?" I asked, assuming this was a purely social call. "We're out of Yoo-hoo, but we have leftover pizza."

"There is no time for the snacks," she said. "We must hurry, before the auntie returns."

She made a beeline for my room and pulled my roller bag out from under the bed, leaving it unzipped on the floor. Then she began grabbing items from my dresser and tossing them into the bag. Her hands moved with certainty as she sorted through my clothes, like she already knew the exact contents of my wardrobe, which she probably did.

"What are you doing?" I asked.

"I pack the suitcase for you."

"But — why? Are we going somewhere?"

"I cannot go. I am the guest yoga instructor this week. You are the one who is going, and you know where it is you go. The Romeo, he is there already, *sí*?"

And then it came to me. "Quinn's in Buenos Aires."

171

"*Por supuesto.* Where is your *pasaporte*? I know you are having one, from when you go to India with the papa. Ah, here it is," she said, opening the drawer of my desk.

Now that I thought about it, it was pretty obvious. Of course Quinn would want to find out for himself once and for all what his father was up to, and he was never going to be able to do that while he was under house arrest in New York.

And my immediate reaction was envy — while I sat around waiting for Natalie to hack Web sites and Rafe to report back on his findings, Quinn had gone ahead and done something. He truly was starring in his own movie.

But that didn't mean I could just pick up and follow him to South America. Quinn was eighteen and had his own money. I was sixteen and had fourteen dollars in my pocket. And at this point I wasn't even supposed to be taking the subway by myself.

"I can't go to Buenos Aires. Charley will kill me. And I have no money."

"You have the ATM? And the credit card, *sí*?"

"*Sí,* I mean, yes, but Patience controls the accounts. She'll cancel the cards if she finds out what I'm doing. And then she'll kill me if Charley hasn't killed me first."

"This is why you go now. You will be in Argentina before they can make you stop."

"But —"

Carolina had been burrowing into the depths of my not very deep closet, but now she spun around and shook a shaming

172

finger in my direction. "Not with the buts. In my country, we do not have the luxury to sit and wait for others to do for us. When we want things to be done, we do them."

She had a point. And the thought of finally taking action was completely intoxicating, not to mention the possibility that I'd actually get to see my mother as soon as the next day.

And that managed to outweigh everything else. I knew Charley would be upset when she found out, but I also hoped she'd understand. She might not agree with Carolina's methods, but I was pretty sure she'd agree with her message.

The time had come to take a starring role.

Twenty-three

Once the decision was made, it was all surprisingly easy, and the fact that it was so easy seemed like an omen, a celestial nod of approval telling me I was doing the right thing. Barely ninety minutes after Carolina buzzed from the street I was at the ticket counter at JFK, booking the last available seat on an overnight flight to Buenos Aires.

There was only one part that didn't feel easy or right, and that was navigating the window of time between when Charley would return to the loft to find me missing and when my flight would take off and she could no longer stop me. I did plan to let her know what I was up to, but I couldn't run the risk of her finding out before I was airborne. Still, I hoped there'd only be an hour or so during which I'd have to worry about Charley worrying about me.

I'd thought about leaving a note back at the loft, but she might discover it too soon — I couldn't let her know the truth until it was too late for her to do anything about it. Instead I'd switched my phone off while I was in the cab on the way to the airport, and I kept it switched off as I waited for my flight to

174

begin boarding. I needed to make sure I couldn't get any calls I didn't want to respond to.

Only at the last possible moment, when I was on the plane and the flight attendant was asking people to power down their cellular devices, did I quickly turn mine back on and text Charley:

> have 2 be star of own movie
> sorry not 2 tell u b4
> rafe will take care of me/no need 2 worry

Then I hit SEND and switched the phone off again, ignoring both the new message icon on the screen and my uneasy conscience as the engines roared into life and the plane lifted off the runway. I'd set my course, and for the next eleven hours, there was nothing anybody could do about it, not even myself.

It turns out that when you buy the single remaining seat on a packed flight, not only is it going to max out your credit limit, it's going to be the least desirable seat on the entire plane, smack in the middle of the very last row, near the lavatories and galley. On one side was a family with three small children squabbling in Spanish and on the other side was a group of people who had nothing in common except their annoyance at being trapped so close to the squabbling children.

So it looked like I was in for an uncomfortable flight, and I'd been in such a rush I hadn't thought to bring a book or my iPod. T.K. would be horrified at the prospect of so much time stretching before me without any potential for educational use, though even she couldn't expect me to try and do physics homework in my current circumstances.

But it didn't matter. Now that I was sitting quietly in one place, the surge of adrenaline that had powered me from the loft to the airport and onto the plane shut down, leaving me exhausted. And in spite of my guilty conscience and the noisy kids and the thunderous snores from a guy a couple of seats away, who'd popped an Ambien while we were still at the gate, I fell into a deep, dreamless sleep.

I awoke to the thump of the wheels hitting the tarmac and applause from some of the passengers. A voice came over the loudspeaker, announcing first in Spanish and then in English our arrival at Ministro Pistarini Airport and informing us that the local time was shortly after seven A.M., an hour ahead of New York. At the end of the row, I could make out a patch of early morning sky through the window.

Around me the other passengers were gathering up their belongings, though it would probably be a while before we reached the gate, and being in the last row meant it would take forever before we could actually disembark. I also noticed a lot of them were turning their phones back on, and I realized the flight attendant must have given permission now that we'd landed. My respite from guilt was officially over.

As my phone powered up, I tried to steel myself for what was to come. I fully expected several dozen outraged texts from Charley, and I also knew she had every right to be outraged. And while I intended to text her back immediately, to assure her I'd arrived safely and would meet up with Rafe as soon as I could get in touch with him, I doubted that would do much to calm her down.

Strangely, though, there were only three messages waiting, which showed a level of restraint that was totally inconsistent with everything I knew about my aunt. The first had a time stamp of 6:17 P.M., about a half hour before my flight had taken off. I could feel the wince already taking shape on my face as I clicked it open:

stopping 4 coffee
text if u need anything or want 2 join
home 7:30ish

So that was a small relief — Charley would've received my own text before she'd even arrived home. There wouldn't have been any window at all of her not knowing where I was.

The time stamp of the next text was 6:39 P.M., and this would inevitably be the outraged one, the response to my text. I opened it quickly, before I could chicken out, and it took me a second to realize it wasn't even from Charley. It was from Natalie instead:

Q's barcode worked
23 Navitaco visitors on day in question
checking names now
shouldn't take long

Which was good news, I thought. Twenty-three was a lot, but once we sorted out the women's names we'd have narrowed things down significantly. Then a simple Internet search should yield enough basic background information to help us figure out if any of them could be La Morena. I texted back an effusive note of thanks before scrolling to the next text.

This final one had a time stamp of 6:48 P.M., so it had to be Charley's furious response, unleashing the full extent of her rage.

But it wasn't. Not at all. It was from Natalie again.

And reading it temporarily put my guilt and Charley's rage completely out of my mind:

ran regression; r-squared at 99% confidence interval

I wasn't quite sure what r-squared meant, but 99 percent confidence sounded good. Particularly when I scrolled down for the rest of the text:

La Morena = Samantha Arquero
Head, Spec Ops, Arquero Energy
Father = Samuel Arquero, President, Arquero Energy

Of course was my first thought.

My second thought was that I should've been able to figure this one out sooner.

I didn't need to run a regression — not that I had any idea how I would anyway. The words on the screen made such perfect sense I felt as if on some subconscious level I'd already known.

And now I was hearing Gwyneth's voice in my head, which was possibly the most bizarre thing that had happened in a while. "My mom will flip," she'd said as she studied the pictures of the EAROFO board. "But I was asking about the old people."

She'd made an interesting point, however unintentionally, and I felt sort of dense for not picking up on it then. After all, every member of the EAROFO board would qualify for the senior discount at the local multiplex. And though this entire situation had been a multigenerational extravaganza, with me orchestrating a search-and-rescue mission for my mother and Quinn's dad being a suspect and everything, it hadn't occurred to any of us to think about the other "children" who might be involved, and specifically EAROFO's next generation.

Meanwhile, if Natalie was 99 percent confident, then I was 100 percent confident, because I had a couple of other data points to throw in, not that Natalie would ever call them data points since they came from Carolina. Regardless, they should push us over the top, even if I didn't have the statistical analysis to prove it.

For starters, Samantha Stephens was the name of the lead character on *Bewitched* — that I knew for sure.

And *arcuarius* was the Latin word for archer, and from there it was just a short skip through various romance languages to get to Arquero as a surname.

So Samantha Arquero was, in fact, *Bewitched* meets the Sagittarius. And as the head of Special Operations for her father's company, she was perfectly situated to play the role of EAROFO's evildoer in chief.

Twenty-four

The plane had arrived at the gate by now, and I could see distant movement as people in the rows closer to the front began to make their way down the aisles. I was literally tapping my foot with impatience, eager to get to work, but I figured I still had at least a few minutes more of being trapped in my seat. It was a seriously enormous plane.

So I hastily sent off another grateful text to Natalie, followed by another apologetic text to Charley to let her know I'd landed without any problems. That I hadn't heard anything further from her was completely ominous — I didn't even want to consider the possibility she was so angry she wasn't speaking to me. But I just told myself there must be a time lag in the phone system somehow, and all of her furious texts would come flooding in at any moment.

The next message I sent was to Rafe, to update him on my whereabouts and coordinate a way to meet up. I was hoping I might actually get to see my mother before the day was out, and maybe before the morning was over. It was even possible I'd get to introduce her to Quinn, and that thought put the uncontrollable smile on my face. Of course, it also assumed I'd ever be able to get off the plane.

"Your first time in Buenos Aires?" the squabbling children's mother asked. Between her needing to mediate their various arguments and my having slept for most of the flight, we hadn't really said anything but "hello" up until then.

"Yes," I told her. And because I thought I should say more if I didn't want to seem unfriendly or like I'd skipped town in a manner that was wholly unauthorized by a parent or legal guardian, I added, "I'm visiting friends." Which was true, sort of, though I was visiting enemies, too, if by visiting you meant hunting them down and exposing their crimes against the environment and my mother.

She smiled. "I am a native, a *porteña*. You will like Buenos Aires. It is a wonderful city, like Paris or Madrid, but with its own flavor." Her English was fluent, with only the faintest trace of an accent, and she began enthusiastically telling me about her favorite sights. I was almost glad I couldn't tell her what I'd really be doing while I was there, because she might be disappointed to hear I'd be too busy to play tourist.

Finally, the rows directly ahead of ours began to empty out. The woman's husband helped me retrieve my roller bag from the overhead compartment, and I followed the whole family down the aisle, along the length of coach, and through first class, where the seats turned into beds and the attendants were still clearing away the remains of a gourmet breakfast. It seemed like the airline wouldn't want the passengers who'd just been crammed into tiny spaces and fed microwaved eggs to see how the more fortunate traveled, but I guess whoever designed the plane didn't worry about class warfare.

Out in the terminal, I was relieved to see the signs were in English as well as Spanish, though I probably could've guessed what *Damas* meant from the skirted stick figure symbol next to the sign. I was sort of a mess, and while I didn't want to waste time, I desperately needed to brush my teeth and wash my face, so I ducked into the ladies' room. The cold water from the tap felt fabulous after having been cooped up for so long in the stale air of the plane, and it was as close as I was going to get to a shower anytime soon.

That done, I followed the signs to immigration, where several hundred other passengers from my flight were already waiting in a long line. Now that I was actually here in Argentina, it seemed unfair that all of my decisive action-taking was resulting in a lot of hanging out and waiting, but I tried to be patient as the line inched forward, checking my phone every so often to see if any new messages had come in yet.

The time crawled by, but eventually I was in front of the bored-looking immigration officer, handing him my passport. "*Buenos días,*" I said, since that was what the flight attendant had said when we'd touched down.

He mumbled something back, not even glancing up as he leafed through my passport until he found the main page with

183

my information and photograph. Then he paused, and his expression shifted abruptly from bored to alert.

I suddenly worried I wasn't old enough to enter the country by myself — I'd been concerned about age restrictions in New York, but it turned out that sixteen was the minimum for purchasing a ticket on one's own, so I'd just passed.

"Cordelia Navare Truesdale," he said slowly, as his eyes moved from the passport page to my face and back again. "That is your name?"

There was something weird about the way he said this — not his English, which was as smooth and accent-free as the woman's on the plane, but his tone and the question itself — and it put me instantly on edge.

"Yes?" I said gingerly.

"Cordelia Navare Truesdale," he said again, turning to the computer next to him and typing on its keyboard. I saw him hit ENTER, and he leaned back, studying whatever popped up on the screen.

After a long moment, he turned away from the computer and gave me another searching look. But then he shook his head, stamped my passport, and handed it over the counter. "Next," he called.

I moved forward with relief, feeling the panic dissipate as I tried to make up for lost time. I zoomed through the baggage claim since I hadn't checked anything and then on through customs and into the arrival hall. Immediately, a dozen different guys approached, all offering transportation into the city, but I figured these were the equivalents of the gypsy cabs in New York and it would be wiser to find an official taxi stand. Besides, I needed to get cash first.

I located an ATM machine along one wall and inserted my card, hoping Charley, enraged as she was, had at least kept Patience in the dark and my account was still active. And it worked fine, though here it offered me Argentinean pesos rather than dollars. I withdrew what I thought was a couple of hundred dollars' worth — pretty much everything I had — and tucked the multicolored bills into my purse.

And as I went to find a taxi, I couldn't help but congratulate myself. After all, I'd gotten myself to a foreign country completely on my own and with relative ease. Even the snag with the guy at immigration hadn't really been a snag. This had to be another sign that I was doing the right thing.

And that's when I saw her.

Samantha Arquero, in the flesh and only fifty feet away.

She was heading for the exit doors, accompanied by a uniformed driver piloting a cart stacked high with Louis Vuitton luggage. She wore a crisply cut pantsuit and her shiny brown hair looked like she'd just had a blowout — she clearly hadn't spent the last eleven hours smushed into the very last row of coach. But it seemed reasonable to assume she had been luxuriating in first class, drinking champagne and nibbling on warm nuts as she plotted further evil.

I stopped short, and at that same moment she did, too, which had me jumping for the protection of a nearby pillar. My heart was beating hard, but I counted to ten and then peeked cautiously around the pillar's side.

But she didn't seem to have noticed me. She'd only paused to look at a flyer taped to a wall, right next to the exit. As I watched, she reached up and peeled the flyer off the wall, studying it closely before folding it and slipping it into her handbag. Then she walked briskly through the doors, accompanied by the driver with her luggage.

I rushed to follow, trying to keep a safe distance between us without losing them altogether. But it turned out these things work better in the movies than they do in real life. I reached the exit just in time to see the driver ushering Samantha Arquero into the backseat of a long, black limousine double-parked at the curb. She disappeared behind its tinted windows and the driver hurried to load her luggage into the trunk. They were pulling away before I'd located the taxi stand, not that I even knew how to say "follow that car" in Spanish. But I was still disappointed that this incredible opportunity had slipped through my hands.

As I waited in what felt like the millionth insanely long line of the day for a taxi, I tried to console myself with the fact that I'd managed to memorize the license plate of the limousine. Fortunately, it was easy to remember: AE-1. I assumed the AE stood for Arquero Energy, which seemed to prove the woman had definitely been Samantha Arquero. And even without the license plate, we should be able to find her again — I mean, how hard could it be to find the Arquero Energy office in Buenos Aires?

Another silver lining was that I wouldn't have to face a lecture from anyone on how it wasn't safe to go chasing after suspects on my own, regardless of how conveniently they'd presented themselves. And I was pretty sure it was nothing more than a coincidence that La Morena and I had been on the same flight. It wasn't like she could've known where I was going when I hadn't even known myself until I was actually on my way.

Anyhow, that thought only reminded me of all the various other people who hadn't known where I was going, along with how I needed to find out where I was heading next, so I took out my phone again, expecting that by now both Rafe and Charley had to have texted me back.

But there were no new messages at all. Only the list of old messages, ending with the final text I'd received from Natalie at 6:49 P.M. the previous evening.

I felt an uncomfortable prickling, the first genuine inkling that something wasn't right. So I clicked over to the outgoing messages screen. The texts I'd written after we'd landed were still there, but each had a little red X next to it, indicating that none had been successfully sent. And that's when I finally figured out what was going on.

With a sinking feeling, I realized Charley hadn't been restrained at all — it was entirely possible she'd texted me thousands of times. In fact, knowing her, she probably had. Her messages just hadn't reached me, for the same reason no other messages had reached me and my own messages hadn't been sent: My phone didn't have international reception.

Twenty-five

I hadn't realized the extent to which my phone served as an electronic security blanket until it was yanked out from under me, but I tried not to freak out. It wasn't like I was in the wilds of Patagonia — in a city of this size there must be a pay phone somewhere. I'd figure out how to work it, get in touch with Charley and Rafe, and everything would be okay.

Regardless, it took until I'd reached the front of the taxi line to calm myself down. Meanwhile, the dispatcher was asking for my *destino*, and I wasn't sure what to tell him. I'd assumed Rafe would text or call with a location for me to meet him, but now I knew that wasn't going to happen. Nor did I know where he was staying or anything useful like that.

But I also couldn't face waiting in line all over again if I gave up my place and went back inside to locate a pay phone — I was wasting too much valuable time, and the point of being here was taking action, not standing around. And I did know where I was likely to find Quinn. At least, I sort of did. I'd head there first, try to connect with him, and then I'd worry about how to get in touch with everyone else.

"He is going to the castle to encounter his papa," Carolina had told me as I zipped my suitcase.

"There's a castle in Buenos Aires?" I'd asked. An image of Sleeping Beauty's castle at Disneyland popped up, unbidden, before my eyes.

"No, not like *La Bella Durmiente*," said Carolina. "It is the name of the hotel where his papa stays."

"The Castle?" That sounded odd, but maybe it was an Argentinean thing and didn't translate well.

"That is what I am seeing," she'd answered in her why-do-you-insist-on-doubting-me-when-I-am-always-right tone.

So I said to the dispatcher, "The Castle Hotel?"

"*Cómo?*" he said, like he'd never heard of such a place.

The guy behind me in line, who'd been demonstrating his impatience by sighing a lot and smoking, leaned in. "*La americana quiere decir palacio, no castillo.*" And then, to me, "You mean the Alvear Palace, *sí*?"

Palace made a lot more sense as the name of a hotel than castle — there was even one in New York — and it was close enough to what Carolina had said that it had to be right. "Is it very expensive?" I asked, just to be sure. I'd seen how Hunter Riley lived in both Southampton and Manhattan, and he wasn't about to stay in a Motel 6.

"*Muy caro*," answered the dispatcher, rubbing his thumb and fingers together in the universal sign of "it will cost you plenty." "The celebrities and the *políticos*, they go there."

"Then, yes, I mean, *sí. Gracias.*"

The taxi didn't look like a New York taxi — it was black with a yellow roof — but otherwise the experience was similar, as if the driver were auditioning for an off-track version of NASCAR that included horn-honking, cursing, and obscene gestures. And if I'd hoped that I might be able to convince him to let me borrow his phone, I was out of luck, because he didn't stop talking on it himself the entire ride except to swear at the other rush-hour drivers. I didn't even get a chance to ask.

Instead I tried to relax and enjoy the scenery as best I could, though the initial part of the drive was along an ordinary-looking highway. But the weather was mild, sunny if a little humid, and when I cracked the window, the breeze felt good on my skin.

It was my first time outside the United States, except for when I was twelve and my dad and I went to India, the year before he died. And I had to admit, I was glad the landscape here had so little in common with Mumbai or New Delhi. That would have only reminded me of our trip together, and how alone I was now.

The driver exited the highway by zooming across several lanes of traffic as the cars he cut off honked in fury. We ended up on an enormous street called the Avenida 9 de Julio, and he began weaving through traffic with a level of aggression that would have been terrifying if I didn't have so much else on my mind and had actually been paying attention.

The avenue's very size suggested July 9 was an important day in Argentinean history, not that I had any idea why, and the driver wasn't exactly giving me a guided tour, though he did stop talking on his phone long enough to point and say, "El Obelisco" as we passed an obelisk rising more than two hundred feet high in the center of a plaza. It looked vaguely familiar, but I didn't know whether that was because it was so much like the Washington Monument or because I'd seen a glimpse of it in the *Evita* clip Charley had played the other night.

Then we turned from the broad avenue onto a series of more regular-sized streets, and the neighborhood began to change. Most of the architecture so far had been relatively nondescript office and apartment buildings, but now I could understand what the woman on the plane had meant about Paris. I'd never been there before, either, but I'd seen pictures, and what I saw here was far more like those pictures than the glass and steel skyscrapers of midtown Manhattan or the converted warehouses of Soho. Most of the buildings looked like they dated back to at least the nineteenth century, constructed of stone with a formal grandeur and careful detailing.

"Recoleta," said the cabdriver, gesturing with a broad flourish, and I guessed this was the name of the area, like Tribeca in New York, though Recoleta was probably more like the Upper East Side. The people on the sidewalks had a cosmopolitan air, smartly dressed in tailored clothing, and elegant mansions and town houses with graceful wrought-iron trim lined the streets. A lot of them appeared to be embassies or other official buildings, but there were also art galleries and restaurants and a bunch of the type of stores Patience shopped at, like Armani and Hermès.

The Alvear Palace was at the corner of Avenida Ayacucho and Avenida Alvear, and its ornate splendor looked completely at home in its fancy surroundings. An assortment of flags fluttered from the broad awning, representing countries ranging from China to Italy to Mexico. More important, I saw the American flag, and since I thought the flags might indicate the nationalities of the guests in residence, I took that as a positive omen.

While I was figuring out how many pesos to give the driver, a doorman hurried to help me out of the taxi and another attendant extracted my bag from the trunk. He began rolling it inside before I finished paying, and I rushed to follow, still wondering if I'd tipped everyone correctly and calling *gracias* over my shoulder.

"You are checking in, yes?" the guy asked as I caught up to him in the entryway. He wasn't much older than me, with friendly brown eyes. A brass nameplate above his breast pocket identified him as Manuel.

"No," I said. And then, "I don't know." Along with all of the other logistical issues I hadn't thought through prior to my arrival in Buenos Aires, I hadn't considered where I'd end up sleeping that night. "Sorry. It's just that I need to find some-one first."

"A guest of the hotel?" Manuel asked, pausing on the blue-and-gold patterned carpet.

"I think so," I said. And then, since my lack of certainty seemed to concern him, I said, "Yes, a guest of the hotel."

He offered to hold my bag at the bell desk while I went to inquire, pointing the way to reception. After my near run-in with Samantha Arquero, I didn't want to accidentally crash into Hunter Riley or any of our other suspects, so I crossed the lobby with caution, keeping an eye out for evildoers.

The decor was imposing and completely over the top — all marble and gilt, with ferns in massive china pots and heavy drap-eries at the windows — and most of the people there seemed to be high-powered businessmen and businesswomen, not that any of them looked familiar. And though Charley had picked out my jeans and Joie embroidered top herself, I still felt incredibly underdressed, young, and awkward as I stepped up to speak to the woman at reception.

Her nameplate said Graciela, and her English was practically better than mine — I was beginning to think everyone in Buenos Aires spoke at least a bit of English, which was a huge relief. "Quinn Riley?" she repeated, trying to find him in her computer. "Do you mean Hunter Riley? We have a guest by that name. Is Quinn traveling with him?"

So I was in the right place, even if Quinn wasn't registered. But when Graciela offered to call up to Hunter's room for me, to see if Quinn was there, that seemed like a really bad idea. Besides everything else, for all I knew, Hunter still thought Quinn was on an entirely different continent, and I wasn't going to be the one to enlighten him. I tried another tack.

"Do you know if anyone's come here looking for Hunter Riley?" I asked. "A youngish guy, maybe, about my age?" *Who's godlike and also happens to be an extremely skilled kisser*, I added, but not out loud.

"I'm afraid I can't discuss our guests or their visitors," Graciela said, but she wasn't mean about it. Then she glanced to either side, to make sure nobody was listening, and in a more conspiratorial tone of voice she said, "I just came on duty, so I wouldn't know. I'm sorry. Perhaps if you check back later?"

I thanked her and told her I would, but I suddenly had a thick feeling in my throat. I'd known that the odds of locating Quinn so easily were low, but it's one thing to tell yourself something and a totally different thing to make yourself feel it. This fresh disappointment threatened to overwhelm me, no matter how sternly I told myself to focus — after all, the clock was ticking, and Quinn or no Quinn, I needed to get in touch with Rafe and Charley.

Manuel was waiting at the bell desk. I swallowed hard before I spoke, but the thick feeling stayed right where it was. "I'm sorry to bother you, but do you know how I can find a pay phone?" I asked him.

"It is not a bother to help such a lovely young lady," he said with a broad smile. There was a business center in the hotel, but it was only for guests, so he suggested I go to a *locutorio*, which was sort of like a phone and Internet café but without the café. He even went over to the concierge and came back with a map, to show me where I could find the nearest one, and then he started telling me how to buy a phone card and make international calls.

And maybe it was because he was being so nice, or maybe it was because I'd been on such an emotional and logistical bender, alternating exhilaration with guilt and confidence with panic and hope with disappointment — anyhow, it all must have taken more of a toll than I'd realized, because Manuel's very kindness had me dangerously close to tears. In fact, one or two might have spilled over before I realized what was happening. I wiped at my cheeks, annoyed with myself.

Even worse, Manuel thought it was his fault. "I have upset you?" he asked, his smile fading.

"No, no — it's not you," I said. And then, because he didn't seem convinced, I tried to explain. "It's only that I made this big decision, to be the star of my own movie and everything, but it's turning into a really bad movie, where nothing happens the way it's supposed to happen."

196

He shrugged in what seemed like a very Latin way. "That is life, yes?" But then he glanced over at the clock above the reception desk. "I can take my break now. I will take you to the *locutorio*, you will tell me about your movie, and I will help you make it end the way you want."

Twenty-six

I had no reason to think Manuel was part of the conspiracy — as coincidences went, that would have been huge, especially since when we formally introduced ourselves he told me he was premed at the University of Buenos Aires and his job at the Alvear was just to cover his living expenses. And it wasn't like I worried about being irresistible — in fact, usually I worried about the exact opposite — but I didn't think he was hitting on me, either. Before we even left the hotel, he'd opened up his wallet to show me a picture of his fiancée, Ana, and another picture of his entire extended family to point out which of his seven nieces he thought I resembled most.

But I'd also learned the hard way that information could be dangerous. T.K. was in her current situation because she knew too much, and that was why Samantha Arquero had tried to get rid of me, too. So as we walked along the Avenida Alvear, I only gave him the most basic version of the story, carefully excising the names of people and companies and organizations like EAROFO and concluding with how I'd come to the hotel hoping to find Quinn.

"It is possible I've seen this young man," Manuel said. "And also his father, if he is a guest of the Alvear. Can you describe them?"

I'd barely begun before he was nodding in recognition. "The son and the father are very similar, no? I have seen them both. The son was across the avenue yesterday afternoon, not doing anything, only waiting and watching the door of the hotel. It was unusual, so I took notice. He was there until the end of my — *cómo se dice*, how long one works?"

"Shift?" I suggested. This was the first time he'd struggled for a word — his English was nearly as perfect as Graciela's.

"Yes, my shift. Then, this morning, when my shift began, he was waiting again. The older man, the father, left the hotel maybe two or three hours before you arrived. He went on foot, so his destination must have been nearby, and the son followed after him."

This news went a long way toward soothing my previous disappointment. Hunter would have to return to the hotel eventually, which meant Quinn would as well, assuming he was still trailing his father. If I couldn't intercept him there myself, I could at least ask Manuel to give him a note.

Meanwhile, the *locutorio* was only a five-minute walk from the Alvear. When I'd started explaining everything to Manuel, he'd offered to lend me his own mobile, but from the way he'd been talking, I had the feeling international calls would be expensive,

199

and it seemed like too much to ask if an alternative was easily available.

Now he led me to what looked like a little store, but there was a green sign out front with symbols for phone and Internet service, and the inside was crowded with phone booths and PC workstations. It was noisy, too, with people chatting to their neighbors as they surfed the net or waited their turn to make calls.

"This is one of the nicer ones," Manuel told me. "Others, they are not so nice. But it is very convenient, no?"

"No. I mean, yes."

Manuel helped me figure out how many pesos I'd need on the debit card I bought, and then he said he'd wait outside. "Are you sure you have time?" I asked. "I don't want to make you late, and I can find my own way back."

"It is my pleasure," he assured me. And then, as if he'd been talking to Rafe or Charley and in spite of having only heard the basic version of events, he added, "You should not be without an escort."

I settled myself on the stool in my cubicle and tried to organize my thoughts as I inserted the debit card into the slot on the phone, readying myself for an onslaught from Charley. The five thousand miles stretching between us might have been a vast physical distance, but it wouldn't offer much of an emotional defense.

Charley was a big fan of caller ID, and she usually opted to screen unfamiliar numbers and also familiar numbers if they belonged to people like Patience. Still, I'd assumed she'd be answering any and all calls until she heard from me, whether she recognized the incoming number or not. Instead, her phone went right into voice mail, like she'd hit IGNORE as soon as it began ringing.

If Charley was ignoring a call that could be from me it meant she was even angrier than I'd thought — which was a terrifying thought — but I left a message anyway. Then I dialed her home number, the one only Carolina and Patience and telemarketers ever used, but the answering machine picked up. It was possible Charley was screening this call, too, but as I left another message there I had a mental image of my voice spilling unheard from the speaker and into the empty loft.

At this point I probably should have just been glad for the temporary reprieve, but it was too unnerving. And when I called Rafe and he didn't answer his phone, either, it was that much more unnerving. I'd thought one if not both of them would be standing by, waiting to take me thoroughly to task before specifying where Rafe would meet me and how I might be able to redeem myself in their eyes once we'd dealt with everything else.

But apparently not.

At least my fourth and final call yielded results. Maybe my day wouldn't be a total waste.

✻   ✻   ✻

When I'd finished, I found Manuel on the sidewalk out front. He'd been talking on his mobile, but he wrapped up his conversation when he saw me. "You were successful?" he asked, returning his phone to his pocket.

"Kind of," I said. "I had to leave a couple of messages when people didn't pick up. I hope you don't mind — you've already done so much — but I told them to call the hotel and ask for you. Is that okay? I didn't know what else to do."

"Certainly it is okay," he said. "I am delighted to be of assistance. We will return immediately."

Now that Manuel knew about the various evildoers loose on the streets of the city, he insisted on checking continuously to see if anyone was following us. And while he'd already been incredibly kind, I was starting to worry that his kindness might present a problem. He seemed to be taking the whole escort thing a bit too seriously, and I had no intention of sitting around the hotel until someone showed up to take his place. It seemed reasonable to check in there first, in case Charley or Rafe had just missed my call and tried back right away, but I was going to have to convince Manuel it would be perfectly safe to venture forth on my own after that.

"Nobody knows I'm here," I reminded him. "Except for people who are on my side, even if they are really angry with me." And the guy at immigration, but I didn't want to think about how creepy that had been.

"True," agreed Manuel. "And it is a very large city. You are like the *aguja en un pajar* — do you have this saying, the needle in the hay —"

He froze, midsentence, in front of a coffeehouse.

"What's wrong —" I started to ask, turning to see what had caught his attention. Though once I did, it wasn't hard to answer my own question.

I'd thought Charley not picking up her phone was unexpected, but I had no idea how to describe something as unexpected as what I saw now. Even if I probably should have expected it, given everything else Dieter had done.

Because there in the window of a café in Buenos Aires, along with a dozen other random flyers for art shows and concerts, was that very same image of Charley and me. It looked like New Yorkers weren't the only ones Dieter had tried to recruit into my personal bodyguard army.

I guessed he'd been too scared of Charley to mention that his brilliant cultural experiment had international dimensions. And I realized that when he'd put his vision into action, it hadn't been completely unreasonable of him to think I might show up in Buenos Aires, not after he'd heard Rafe and Charley and me discussing the investigation and debating next steps. In a way, it had actually been impressive planning on his part — prescient even. But somehow it all felt much less yellow here.

Because suddenly the creepiness of the guy at immigration made a lot more sense. He hadn't been trying to determine if my passport was a fake. He'd been trying to put a name to a face, and specifically my name to my face, since he'd seen my face before.

And now I also had a pretty good idea of what Samantha Arquero had removed from the wall in the airport. I wondered what she'd made of it — after all, she had no way of knowing Dieter's intentions.

Regardless, it was starting to seem like the relative anonymity I'd been counting on might not be such a safe thing to count on. I was still like an *aguja en un pajar*, except the *pajar* was wallpapered with my picture.

Anyhow, I ended up telling Manuel about mobilizing the power of the masses, which he reacted to with a skepticism that also seemed very Latin, so after that we started talking about the differences between New Yorkers and *porteños*, and then he began telling me a bit about Buenos Aires history, and before I knew it we were approaching the hotel's side entrance.

I thanked him again. "I would have been lost without your help, Manuel."

"It was nothing," he said. "But you are very welcome. And we are friends now, and my friends call me Manolo, so you must do the same."

"I'd like that," I said. "Thank you, Manolo." He'd been so nice I wanted to hug him, but I wasn't sure how Argentineans felt about their personal space. Instead, I awkwardly stuck out my hand.

He laughed. "Handshakes are for Americans. This is how *porteños* say hello and good-bye to their friends." And he leaned down to kiss me once, on my right cheek.

It was really more of a peck than a kiss, completely harmless and not all that different from Patience's air kisses. So when he indicated I should do the same to him, I stood on tiptoe and pecked his right cheek.

And then someone spoke a single word from behind us.

"Ahem."

Twenty-seven

When I saw Quinn, standing there in the same dark green sweater he'd been wearing at the museum, the urge to throw myself at him was even stronger than the brain paralysis.

There was just one small problem: He didn't look anywhere near as happy to see me as I was to see him. In fact, he looked sort of grim, possibly because he hadn't received his own tutorial on Buenos Aires culture and as far as he knew, I'd just been kissing a total stranger.

Of course, from his angle he probably couldn't tell it was only an air kiss, and a pathetic part of me was thrilled he cared enough to be jealous, assuming that was what was going on. After all, Quinn could be angry for some other reason entirely.

Either way, Manolo came to my rescue yet again. At least, he tried.

"I am Manolo," he said with his broad smile. "And you must be Quinn. Delia has told me a great deal about you. I feel we are friends already."

And with that he planted a big kiss on Quinn's right cheek. Then he gave me the least subtle wink I'd ever seen and disappeared into the hotel.

206

"That's how *porteños* say hello and good-bye," I told Quinn. And because he still hadn't said anything, I kept going. "People from Buenos Aires call themselves *porteños*. Because it's a port. On the Río de la Plata. Which isn't actually a river but an estuary, like the lower half of the Hudson. But they call it a river anyway. Manolo was telling me about it."

"I bet he was," said Quinn, and there was a dangerous edge to his voice.

And maybe it was the edge that did it. He still looked every bit as grim, but I threw myself at him anyway.

"I can't believe Charley let you come here by yourself," he said eventually.

"She didn't exactly let me," I confessed. "It was Carolina's idea."

Quinn knew exactly how Charley felt about Carolina and her ideas. "Charley's going to kill you," he said. "And I'm glad to see you and everything, but I don't think anyone would blame her if she did."

"I'm hoping she'll be over it before I get back. Besides, it's not like you had permission, either."

"I left Fiona a note."

"Well, I sent Charley a text."

"You ran away by text?"

"I didn't run away. I went on a mission. It's different. And I don't see how a text is worse than a note."

207

"It's not, but nobody's out to get me," he said.

"If you think about it, it's almost safer here. The people who are out to get me all think I'm in New York. Everyone does, apart from Charley and Rafe and Carolina. What about you? Who knows where you are?"

"Only you. And that guy who just kissed us."

After we'd explained a few more things to each other, we went inside to check with Manolo, but nobody had left any messages. And now that I'd found Quinn, I didn't have to worry about Manolo thinking he needed to keep an eye on me.

He did, however, suggest Quinn and I get some lunch before we made our next move, which seemed like a good idea. Even though we had a lot to do, my last meal was a hazy memory from a distant continent, and once I started thinking about food it was nearly impossible to think about anything else.

Manolo got another map from the concierge and traced a route for us to a tiny restaurant on a street called Posadas. There were just twelve tables inside, and as far as we could tell we were the only nonnatives in the place, which we decided meant it was authentically Argentinean. And since everyone was eating empanadas, that's what we ordered as well.

I'd had empanadas a couple of times before, from a street vendor near Charley's apartment, and they'd been okay — sort of like the South American version of Indian samosas or Italian calzones. The ones here, however, were closer to an art form — pockets of flaky pastry crust filled with spiced meat or corn or cheese and completely delicious. I inhaled mine and helped Quinn finish his when he ordered seconds.

So the empanadas were a totally welcome experience, and in the process of being seated and ordering and everything I also made another important discovery: Quinn spoke Spanish, not just from taking it at school but from when he'd gone to surfing camp in Baja. And while I knew I should focus on the practical benefits of having a Spanish speaker around, as I watched him talk to the waiter, rolling his *r*'s like it was a perfectly natural thing to do, I was mostly just amazed by how it made him seem even more godlike. I wouldn't have thought such a thing was possible if I didn't have the evidence right in front of me.

Anyhow, as we ate I caught him up on everything I'd learned since Saturday afternoon. This pretty much came down to La Morena being Samantha Arquero and that she was in Buenos Aires at that very moment, along with everyone else.

Then it was Quinn's turn to update me. And for his sake, I'd been hoping he'd learned something about his father's activities that would prove we were wrong to suspect him. But judging by the way he pushed aside the remaining empanada and the shutdown look that came over his face as he began to speak, Hunter hadn't been up to anything good.

"My flight got in around noon yesterday, and as soon as I landed I went straight to my dad's hotel," Quinn said. "I called his room from the lobby, and he answered, so I knew he was there, but I didn't want to confront him — I was worried he'd

209

only deny everything and try to send me home. Instead I hung up without saying anything and figured I'd wait for him to leave and then follow wherever he went. Not that he went anywhere at first. It was a serious drag — I <u>was</u> across the street, just watching, for the whole afternoon. Finally, though, right when it was getting dark, he came out and started walking. He didn't even notice I was right behind him."

"Where did he go?" I asked.

"The European Commission's delegation to Argentina."

"What's that?"

"The European Commission is the executive branch of the European Union, and its headquarters are in a building not far from the hotel. I looked it up online — it represents the interests of all of the major European countries and most of the minor ones, too."

I tried to process this. "What's your father doing with the European Union?"

"It's not just the European Union. This morning, I followed him to the Russian Embassy, and after that he was picked up by a car with diplomatic plates for the Japanese Embassy. I lost him then — I couldn't find a cab fast enough. But that was okay. I'd already seen everything I needed to see."

"The European Union, Russia, and Japan?"

"He probably hit up a bunch of other countries, too, before I even got here."

"Is he hoping the different governments will invest in his hedge fund?" I couldn't help it — I was still looking for a way to clear Hunter's name, and that was the only legitimate reason I could think of for Quinn's father to be acting like the United Nations social chair.

"I wish," said Quinn. "His fund's closed — that means he's not taking new investors, he's only managing the money he already has. Besides, if that were the case, he'd have no reason to hide it from people in his office or Fiona. No, I think the real answer is a lot simpler."

"How simple?"

"We've been talking all along about how EAROFO must be paying off the different international organizations that are supposed to enforce the antidrilling treaties. And I think that's where Hunter comes in. He's the guy in the middle. He's somehow greasing the palms of the regulators and watchdogs, and in exchange EAROFO is giving him privileged information."

"Oh," I said, letting that sink in. It did make sense. In fact, it explained a lot.

But I also hated the way Quinn sounded, like he'd been drained of anything positive or hopeful. "There could be another explanation," I said, not that one was exactly springing to mind.

"Another explanation for why Hunter knows all of the EAROFO people, has that spreadsheet on his computer, and is arranging secret meetings with government agencies in foreign countries?" He motioned for the check and then turned back to me. His eyes were even grayer now than they'd been at the museum. "Do you know what the worst part is?" he asked.

I shook my head.

"I came down here still hoping Hunter was a good guy. I mean, he gets on my case about certain things, but only because he cares. And with my mom the way she was, the way she is, he had an extra space to fill, but he always managed to fill it. I know that at some point everybody has to realize parents are human and flawed and everything, and it's not like I ever thought he was perfect, but I just couldn't make myself believe he was as flawed as this. I actually thought I'd find out there really was another explanation, an explanation that would make it all right. But it's not all right. It will never be right."

And I couldn't think of anything to say to that.

Twenty-eight

The break for empanadas and debriefing had been very necessary, but it was well past two o'clock when we left the restaurant, and we'd have to rush.

There was a pay phone on a nearby corner, and while it wasn't exactly private, it was fine for making a quick call to check in with Manolo, especially since it turned out he had nothing new to report. His shift would be ending soon, too, but he'd arranged for a friend on the hotel switchboard to take messages on my behalf should anybody call once he'd gone off duty. So we were covered on that front.

Still, I couldn't help feeling even more unsettled than ever as I thanked him and said good-bye — at this point, it had been almost three hours with no response from Charley or Rafe. It was frustrating that I was no closer to seeing T.K., but I was also beginning to worry something had gone seriously wrong, and I didn't know what that something could be, much less what I should do about it except stick to my current plan.

First, though, we had an important errand to attend to. Quinn had come prepared, and he pulled a knit cap and sunglasses from his backpack and put them on as we left the restaurant. This mostly made him look like a celebrity trying to keep a low profile — just the other day I'd spotted Robert Pattinson on West Broadway in an almost identical getup — but being mistaken for a celebrity in incognito mode was better than being recognized for who he really was should we accidentally cross Hunter's path.

I, however, had come a lot less prepared — Carolina's idea of packing involved stuffing anything pink or purple into my suitcase — and now I needed a disguise of my own. Quinn had spoken to the maître d' at the restaurant, and based on his directions we headed along Posadas and cut through a small park.

It was a gorgeous day, sunny with a slight breeze, and while in New York the leaves were already starting to turn, here it was spring — the flower beds were bright with color and wild parrots squawked in the branches of the rubber trees. We turned onto the Avenida Junín, passing the Basílica Nuestra Señora del Pilar, an elegant baroque church painted a gleaming white, and then the gates to the Cementerio de la Recoleta, an enormous cemetery where everybody who was anybody in Buenos Aires went to be buried, including the real Evita.

Judging by the buses parked on the street and the people with cameras swarming around, the Basílica and the cemetery were major tourist attractions, and if we'd had time we probably would've stopped to check them out. But we weren't there for the sights — our destination was the collection of sidewalk stands catering to the tourists. And across from the cemetery gates we found exactly what we were looking for: a guy selling hats.

Sadly, his selection was geared toward people's souvenir needs, and specifically the needs of people who for whatever reason wanted to dress like gauchos. Gauchos were the Argentinean version of cowboys, and apparently they favored hats made of wool felt, with wide brims and attractive chinstraps for when their wearers were galloping across the pampas.

I doubted Charley would approve of the fashion statement I'd be making, but the price was right, and coming here had been more efficient than trying to find a shopping mall. And at least I could find a hat that fit my tiny head, since a lot of the stock was in children's sizes. We chose one with a brim that came down far enough to hide most of my face while still allowing me to see, and after adding a cheap pair of mirrored sunglasses my disguise was complete. Of course, I was also pretty sure I looked like a total idiot no matter what Quinn said, but it seemed like a small sacrifice given the circumstances.

That done, we hailed a passing cab. We had an appointment of sorts, one I'd set up with the final phone call I'd made at the *locutorio*. "El Obelisco, *por favor*," Quinn told the driver with fluent ease.

The Alvear made sense as a base of operations for Hunter since so many of the embassies were close by, but I'd wanted a more action-packed setting for what was going to happen next, and the monument had been the first thing to come to mind when I'd been making arrangements. To be honest, it was the only thing that came to mind — I wasn't exactly well versed in local landmarks.

The driver gunned his engine and plunged into traffic with an utter disregard for the other cars on the road, traffic signals, and stray pedestrians. He was also as busy on his cell phone as the driver I'd had earlier, so if we were passing anything interesting, we had to figure it out for ourselves.

Quinn could read in a moving vehicle without getting carsick, and he studied our map as the driver alternated between flooring it and slamming on the brakes. "That's the Palacio de Justicia, which I think is the Supreme Court," he said, when a pillared building flashed by, "and that's a really famous synagogue," he added, gesturing to a blur of carved Byzantine facade. Then, as we zipped by a stately Renaissance structure topped with a triangular pediment, he said, "That's the Teatro Colón. It's like the Lincoln Center of Buenos Aires."

So the trip was moderately educational, and learning what everything was distracted us from the fact that the driver seemed to have a death wish. A couple of blocks beyond the Teatro Colón he screeched to a stop at the edge of the Plaza de la República, the mammoth oval where the twelve lanes of Avenida 9 de Julio met the six lanes of Avenida Corrientes. In the middle, El Obelisco rose from a grassy island the size of a football field.

We'd arrived with ten minutes to spare, and we needed five of them just to cross the crazed traffic between us and the center island. Then we had to find a spot that offered a clear view of people coming and going and where it wouldn't be immediately obvious we were on a stakeout.

"Too bad we don't have a camera," I said. "We could pretend to be tourists."

"We do have a camera," said Quinn, digging one out of his backpack. "I thought it might come in handy. It has a zoom feature, though it's no substitute for binoculars. I've got binoculars, too, with great aspherical lenses, but those might attract unwanted attention."

He'd definitely put more thought into packing for this trip than Carolina and I had. "What else do you have in there?" I asked.

"Toothbrush, toothpaste. Change of clothes. My iPod. A book or two. Various surveillance equipment."

"Wait — what?"

"Surveillance equipment. You know, like the binoculars, and a pen that's actually a video recorder, and a bionic ear, which lets you listen in on people's conversations — basic stuff like that."

"You just happened to have all that lying around your house?"

He sounded almost sheepish as he explained. "When I was little, maybe Bea's age, I got really into James Bond. It was sort of how my dad and I bonded. Hunter's a huge fan. He's collected

217

first editions of all of Ian Fleming's books — that's the guy who created Bond — and on birthdays and holidays he always gives me secret agent–type gadgets. So, yeah, I did have all this stuff lying around."

The way Quinn and Hunter were about James Bond wasn't that different from how Ash and I had been about surfing — I didn't think he should be embarrassed. Before I could say anything, though, Quinn grabbed my arm. "Is that him?" he asked.

I turned. And sure enough, there was Thad, threading his way through the six lanes on the other side of the avenue. Quinn had never met him before, but in his khakis and button-down shirt, and with his BlackBerry clipped to his waist, Thad looked exactly like what he was — a tech executive from Silicon Valley — so here in Buenos Aires he didn't exactly melt into the crowd. As we watched, he narrowly escaped being flattened by a truck running the red light, and I couldn't help registering a twinge of disappointment.

He managed to reach the center island intact and began scanning the crowd, searching for a specific face. Even without the hat and sunglasses he probably wouldn't have noticed me — after all, he didn't expect me to be there, and he was looking for someone else entirely — but I was glad of my disguise and Quinn's presence as his eyes passed over us.

When I'd called Brett from the *locutorio*, she said she'd do what she could, but she also warned me Thad had been less than responsive to the messages she'd already sent while he'd been away.

Still, it looked like an urgent request to meet Samantha Arquero at the Obelisk at 3:30 P.M. was all it took to get his attention.

Regardless, I was stunned my plan had worked. Not only had I confirmed there was a connection between Thad and Samantha Arquero — why else would her name be sufficient to lure him here? — but now we could also follow him wherever he went next.

Thad, meanwhile, had no way of knowing Samantha Arquero wouldn't arrive at any moment, and he settled in to wait for her. For him this meant fiddling with his BlackBerry and glancing up every few seconds to see if she'd appeared. Fifty feet away and safely off to the side, out of his line of vision, Quinn and I pretended to be busy taking pictures.

A full fifteen minutes elapsed before it seemed to occur to Thad that he might have been stood up. Through the camera's zoom lens, I could see his expression in profile, morphing from impatient and weaselish to annoyed and weaselish. He took a wireless headset from his pocket and clipped it to his ear before thumbing something into his BlackBerry.

"Perfect," said Quinn, grabbing a cell phone from his backpack.

Only it wasn't really a cell phone — it just looked like one. "My dad gave me this for Christmas last year," he explained in a

219

low voice, pulling off his sunglasses so he could get a better look at its screen and pushing buttons on its keypad. "It lets you tap into other people's Bluetooth connections up to a twenty-five-yard radius. You can hear both sides of their call, but they can't hear you."

And the amazing thing was that it worked. When Quinn held the phone to my ear, bending down so we could listen together, there was the sound of a number being dialed and then someone answering.

"Arquero Energía Argentina," announced a woman's voice.

"Samantha Arquero, *por favor.*" This voice was Thad's, and it was as clear as if he'd called us directly, though his Spanish didn't sound anywhere near as good as Quinn's.

"*Momento,*" came the response.

And a moment later, another woman came on the line. "*La oficina de* Samantha Arquero," she said.

"Teresa, it's Thad Wilcox. I've been waiting for Ms. Arquero for fifteen minutes. Where is she?"

"Oh, hello, Mr. Wilcox," the woman answered, a note of confusion in her tone. "Ms. Arquero is in a conference with her father this afternoon."

"I had a message from my assistant to meet her at three thirty," Thad insisted.

"I'm afraid there has been a mistake. You are on her schedule for tomorrow morning, as we arranged last week. I was going to call you at the end of the day to reconfirm. Eleven o'clock at the Café Tortoni."

Thad hung up without saying thank you or good-bye, and then he immediately dialed a new number. Quinn and I listened as it rang four times before a voice mail greeting clicked on.

This is Brett Fitzgerald at TrueTech. I'm on the other line
or away from my desk. Please leave your name and number,
and I'll return your call as soon as I can.

Thad gave an irritated grunt as he waited for the beep. "Terrific," he said sarcastically. "You're probably out at lunch already, and it's not even noon yet in California. I need to know about that urgent message from Samantha Arquero. Call me ASAP. And I mean ASAP."

He ended this call as ceremoniously as he'd ended the previous one and yanked the headset from his ear. He shoved it into his pocket and clipped his BlackBerry back onto his belt as he strode over to the crosswalk and waited impatiently for the light to change. I felt guilty about Brett — I should have realized Thad would call to check when Samantha Arquero didn't appear. And based on how angry he'd sounded, I wouldn't put it past him to fire her. I could reassure myself that my mother would fix everything once she returned, but Brett didn't know that, and I couldn't tell her until it was actually safe for T.K. to come back.

The green light finally turned red and the DON'T WALK signal gave way to the WALK signal. Quinn and I moved to follow Thad as he stepped into the street, trying to keep a safe distance behind.

But before he was even halfway across, Thad froze in his tracks, right there in the crosswalk. Then he spun around, and the look on his face reminded me of a cartoon character who'd just had an epiphany. There should have been a bubble above his head with a lightbulb inside.

He headed back for the center island, and now he wasn't even watching for the occasional rogue driver who might decide to ignore the red light. Instead, he was scanning the people around the Obelisk with fresh intensity.

Fortunately, Quinn and I hadn't even made it to the crosswalk yet, and my disguise was still in place. Now we paused and feigned immersion in our map. From the corner of my eye, though, I could see Thad's gaze sweep over us as he stalked by, and he was clipping his headset back onto his ear.

"He's making another call," I whispered to Quinn, who was already punching buttons on the spy phone.

We had a false start, picking up the signal from some unknown person's phone instead, but Quinn pressed another button and the torrent of Spanish was replaced with another annoyed grunt from Thad as his call was answered by voice mail.

For a fleeting moment, I thought he'd tried to reach Brett again, and that this time he really would fire her — not only over the phone, but by leaving a message, which seemed extra wrong.

But the greeting that picked up wasn't Brett's.

It was mine.

Twenty-nine

I'd recorded the greeting months and months ago, long before T.K. had disappeared and my entire life exploded. As I listened to my own voice, it sounded strangely sunny and carefree, like a relic of a different person altogether.

> *Hi. It's Delia. Sorry I missed you. Leave a message, and I'll call you back.*

And then, like a true Californian, I added: "Have a great day!" I couldn't believe Charley hadn't made me change that — people telling her what kind of day to have was right up there with emoticons on her list of pet peeves.

Thad, however, didn't sound like he was having a great day as he recorded his message. In fact, he sounded like he was having a really bad day. "Delia. This is Thad Wilcox. I'm wondering where you are right now. I suspect it's not where you're supposed to be."

There was an undertone of menace to his words that was more than a little disturbing, though he was less condescending than he'd been when he threatened me in Patience's apartment the previous week — maybe he was starting to respect me, now that he knew I could scheme and connive, too.

Because though it had taken him a while, it seemed safe to assume he'd realized I might have been behind the message about Samantha Arquero. After all, who else would have used Brett as a go-between? Samantha Arquero's assistant sounded like she was used to talking to Thad directly — he'd known her name and everything.

And if Thad had figured that out, he'd probably also figured out there was a decent chance I was somewhere nearby, hoping to do exactly what I'd been hoping to do. My brilliant plan was starting to look a lot less brilliant.

Especially since as he continued to speak, something weird began happening to our spy phone connection, kind of like an echo effect.

Except it wasn't an echo.

Slowly, trying not to give us away with any abrupt movement, I turned my head to get a better look. Thad was moving in our direction, and now we could hear him in stereo, both through the spy phone and more faintly as his voice traveled toward us, carried on the breeze.

He was still a healthy distance away, searching the faces of everyone he passed, so I didn't think he'd spotted us.

"We should get out of here," said Quinn softly, closing the spy phone and slipping it into his bag.

"Good idea," I said. Quinn put his arm around my

shoulders in a casual, touristlike gesture, and we started for the crosswalk.

And that's when it happened. A sudden gust of wind caught the brim of my hat, and because I'd drawn the line at actually using the chinstrap, it went spinning off my head. My hair whipped around my face, so I couldn't even see, but I heard Thad give a shout of discovery. "Delia!"

There was no time to wait for the light to change. Quinn grabbed my hand, and we dove into traffic.

The next thirty seconds were the longest of my life, since I fully expected each one would be my last. None of the surfing or snowboarding or anything I'd done with Ash had prepared me for sprinting across six lanes' worth of speeding traffic, though it would have made a riveting new X Games event.

Taxis and motorcycles and trucks rushed at us in a dizzying assault of color and speed and noise as we darted from lane to lane, their horns blaring in protest. It was probably a good thing I didn't know Spanish, because I had the feeling every single one of the words the drivers were throwing out at us would be bleeped if they ended up on TV.

I still don't know how we reached the other side without becoming roadkill, but somehow we made it. And I could tell from the way the yelling and honking continued behind us that Thad was giving chase.

The restaurants and theaters and cafés along the Avenida Corrientes were a blur of stone and glass as we ran past, dodging the pedestrians on the sidewalk and dashing across another intersection just as the signal changed.

Of course, after crossing the enormous Avenida 9 de Julio against the light, a regular street wasn't much of a challenge — it didn't stop us and it didn't stop Thad. When we looked back, he was still on our heels, weaving through oncoming traffic. Even the shriek of metal upon metal as a car swerved to avoid him and smashed into a parked van wasn't enough to break his stride.

I was pretty fast for my size and the adrenaline pumping through me definitely helped, but I knew Quinn had slowed to match my pace, and Thad's legs were a lot longer than mine. Thad also wasn't wearing the Christian Louboutin ankle boots Charley had insisted were the only possible footwear for the jeans I had on, not that she'd been factoring in the potential for impromptu track meets.

We made the light again at the next intersection, and the next, but every time I stole a glance over my shoulder the gap between us and Thad seemed to narrow. It was like the most clichéd nightmare there was — being chased through the streets of an unfamiliar city, with the pounding footsteps drawing ever closer — but this was real and in broad daylight.

The fourth intersection we came to was the Avenida Florida, a pedestrian zone thronged with shoppers and tourists, all enjoying the spring afternoon. Quinn and I were thinking and moving like one person, and we automatically cut right and into the crowd. The lag between when we turned the corner and when

Thad did might buy us just enough time out of his sight to lose him. Particularly if he didn't see us race into one of the dozens of shops lining the street.

At the last possible moment, we cut right again and through a set of doors.

We found ourselves in a bookstore, its quiet calm in jarring contrast to the frenzy of the last five minutes. And if the customers inside thought two American teenagers bursting in and immediately crouching down behind a table stacked with paperbacks was odd, none of them showed it. Mostly they were too absorbed examining the books and magazines on display to pay any attention to us. Nor did they notice Thad moments later, hurtling past on the street outside. Quinn and I watched, peering over the stacked books and through the window, as he elbowed his way through the people milling about, pushing forward as if he thought we were still ahead of him.

Several doors down, though, he came to an abrupt halt. Panting, he put his hands on his hips and turned in a slow circle, surveying the crowd and the storefronts.

For once I was glad I was so short, pinhead and all. Thad knew how easy it would be for me to slip away, shielded by the height of others. And the brilliant sun reflecting off the glass turned the shop windows into mirrors, making it impossible to see who might be hiding within. We could have been anywhere, inside or out. But my heart was still beating incredibly fast, and not just from the running.

Thad turned in another slow circle, breathing hard, and then another, but on his next trip around something caught his attention and he did a double take. He was facing away from us, but I ducked down further behind our bookshelf anyway. And when I peeked over the books again, he was staring at a kiosk papered with flyers and ads. As I watched, he walked over, and with an angry tug he ripped off one of the flyers and tore it to pieces.

There was no way to see what was on the flyer, but at this point I could be pretty confident it was another part of Dieter's cultural experiment. And if Thad's familiarity with Samantha Arquero and how he'd just tried to chase me down hadn't been enough to prove which side he was on, watching him tear my image to shreds was the clincher.

Either way, he'd apparently resigned himself to temporary defeat. He tossed the remnants of the flyer to the ground and trudged off, returning in the direction of Avenida Corrientes and disappearing from sight.

He'd lost us, but we knew exactly where we'd be able to find him.

And miraculously, Quinn was still holding my hand.

229

Thirty

We hung out in the bookstore a while longer, to catch our breath and make sure Thad was truly gone. The sales clerk pointed me to a pay phone in the back, and I left Quinn browsing guidebooks and went to check in with the switchboard at the Alvear again. I'd memorized the number by now, and when the operator answered, I asked for Lourdes, as Manolo had instructed.

Lourdes was expecting my call. "You are the new friend of Manolo, sí? He is *muy simpático*, Manolo, always with the new friends. He is studying to be a doctor, you know." She was as proud as if he were her grandson.

Anyhow, after Lourdes and I talked some more about how much we liked Manolo, I asked if anyone had called for me.

"Yes, indeed," she said happily, and my heart skipped a beat — in a nice way for once. "I have the message here, from a Señor Rafael Francisco Valenzuela Sáenz de Santamaría. He is your uncle?"

That seemed optimistic on Rafe's part. He might be completely smitten with Charley, but it would be a stretch to construe their current relationship as even dating — the odds of him becoming my uncle anytime soon were low. But I went with it anyway. "Right, my uncle. What did he say?"

"He is very mysterious, your uncle. He says to tell you he has found the captain's elected tail. Do you know what this means?"

Assuming Rafe had actually said electronic, not elected, and trail, not tail, I did know what it meant, and that was good news, because it would help us nail Samantha Arquero. "Did he mention where he was? Or where anyone else was?" Like T.K., for instance, though I didn't really think Rafe would divulge her whereabouts over the phone to a total stranger, however grandmotherly she sounded.

"No, he only said to tell you he would be on a plane tonight, but you should return to the hotel. This is very important. He was very clear on this topic."

"Okay," I said, which wasn't technically lying, since I'd have to return to the hotel eventually — my suitcase was there, after all. "If he calls back, would you mind telling him I'm with Quinn, everything's fine, and he shouldn't worry?" I asked.

"Certainly," she said.

It was reassuring to have heard from Rafe, but it didn't make me feel any better about the continued silence from Charley. So after I'd finished thanking Lourdes, I disconnected and tried her directly. The balance on my card was getting low, and I watched the pesos tick down on the phone's screen as I dialed, hoping I had enough money for the call.

But it didn't matter. Charley's number went straight into voice mail again.

Not only had Quinn and I entirely escaped injury, we both still had our belongings with us — all except for my hat. And while I couldn't say I'd miss that specific hat, I did need to find a replacement if I didn't want to feel totally exposed out on the street. After what had happened with Thad, I preferred a tangible disguise to the intangible power of the masses.

Quinn's new guidebook directed us to the Galerías Pacífico, a few blocks away on Avenida Florida. This was a fancy shopping arcade with a high, frescoed ceiling stretching above the tiers of stores. It made the mall in Palo Alto look as if it had been constructed from cardboard boxes, but I guessed the developer there was less concerned about charm than the guy who'd built this place.

In a small boutique, I found a fedora that just might be worthy of Charley's approval, and Quinn picked one out, too. I appreciated the gesture of solidarity, but I was starting to think it was useless for him to try to disguise himself — he looked as much like a movie star in the fedora as he had in the knit cap. He also insisted on paying for everything, since in addition to his surveillance equipment, he'd brought a wad of cash, though I knew T.K. or Charley or whichever relative I saw next would be equally insistent about paying him back.

"Now what?" he said.

At this point, I'd already reconciled myself to the fact that I wasn't going to see my mother until Rafe returned to Buenos Aires. We could try to track down Samantha Arquero, but that seemed like asking for trouble when we'd been handed such a golden opportunity to ambush her meeting with Thad the next morning instead. Meanwhile, Quinn had solved the Hunter mystery for himself, so it wasn't like we needed to pursue it any further, at least not for the time being. "We're sort of done for the day," I said.

"Then let's make the most of it," said Quinn.

He didn't add "while we can," though the thought of what tomorrow might hold was there, hovering over us both.

So we played tourist for the rest of the afternoon, sight-seeing our way to the Plaza de Mayo, a large square edged by the Casa Rosada, the pinkish building with the balcony where Madonna sang "Don't Cry for Me Argentina" in the *Evita* clip — apparently real politicians made speeches there, too — and the Cabildo, which had housed the government when Argentina was a Spanish colony, more than two hundred years ago. With its double row of white-painted arches and bell tower, it reminded me of mission-style buildings back in California, which made sense since the Spanish had been there, too, way back when. After that, we wandered through San Telmo, one of Buenos Aires's oldest neighborhoods, with narrow cobblestoned streets and lots of little cafés and antique shops.

And maybe it was the very foreignness of the city — the centuries-old buildings and the exotic rhythm of the Spanish spoken around us and the slightly tropical feel to the air — but it was like we'd stepped out of our regular lives. I couldn't forget completely why we were there, but it all felt very far away.

As the afternoon faded into evening, we found a *parrilla* for another authentically Argentinean meal. *Parrilla* means "grilled meat" in Spanish, so this was essentially a steak house. According to the guidebook, Argentina has the highest per capita meat consumption in the world, and it would probably be a really bad place to be a vegetarian. Fortunately, both Quinn and I were omnivores, because the steak we ordered was the best I'd ever had, and the little salads that came beforehand were delicious, too.

"That was incredible," I said when I'd finished everything on my plate. I didn't even have room for ice cream.

"It was," Quinn agreed, checking his watch. "But we should get going."

I hadn't realized we had any after-dinner plans. "What did you have in mind?"

Quinn didn't answer but just led me out of the restaurant and into a cab, giving the driver an address a short drive away. We pulled up near one of the corners we'd sprinted by that afternoon, only Thad was nowhere in sight this time around.

Out on the sidewalk, Quinn paused in front of a door set

with panes of frosted glass. "Before we go inside, you have to promise me something."

"Anything," I said.

"I'm serious," he said, though his tone was actually sort of joking.

"So am I."

"What happens here, stays here."

"Okay. What happens here?"

"You'll see. But if anyone at school ever finds out, I'll never hear the end of it. My image will be shot."

"Even more than if they find out about your James Bond complex?"

He laughed. "That might have to stay here, too. So, you promise?"

"I promise," I said.

He pulled the door open, and we stepped into a reception area with dark paneled walls and a marble staircase at the far end. There was a desk to one side, and Quinn went to speak to the attendant. I couldn't understand what they said — it was all in Spanish — but Quinn handed over some pesos and we checked our hats and bags before heading upstairs.

The hum of voices grew louder as we climbed to the second floor. I thought maybe we were going to a nightclub, though I didn't hear the thumping bass of house music, and the faded grandeur of our surroundings was nothing like any club I'd seen in the movies or on TV. Instead we passed through a set of French doors and into an old-fashioned ballroom.

The chandeliers and deep red of the walls lent a warm glow to the room, mellowing the features of everyone gathered around the dance floor. There must have been more than a hundred people, ranging from our age to a few who might have been in their eighties or even nineties, all chatting and laughing as a small orchestra tuned its instruments on a bandstand. Most of the men were dressed in suits and ties, and a lot of the women wore evening dresses and brightly colored flowers in their hair.

"What is this?" I asked Quinn.

"*Milonga,*" he said.

And as if on cue, the orchestra's conductor tapped his baton. The crowd stopped milling about and rearranged itself into ready pairs on the dance floor.

Then the music started to play, led by a dramatic, melancholy violin, and the room came alive with tango.

Thirty-one

I looked up at Quinn in wonder.

"Argentina's famous for tango," he said, trying, not very successfully, to sound like bringing me here wasn't a big deal when it was actually the most romantic thing that had ever happened to anyone in the history of romance. "I asked the guy at the bookstore, while you were on the phone, and he suggested this place."

"Did James Bond tango?"

Quinn didn't skip a beat. "In *Never Say Never Again*."

It was gorgeous to watch — some of the dancers could have been professionals, gliding across the floor with fluid grace — but it was also impossible not to join in. Of course, neither of us knew what we were doing, so we blundered along, trying our best to imitate the couples around us without getting in their way.

We probably looked terrible next to the people who really did know what they were doing, and in my jeans I could never match the elegance of the women in their flowing dresses, but it didn't seem to matter.

And somehow, at least for a little while, the messy, disturbing circumstances that had brought us to that ballroom at that moment in time melted away, leaving only the music and the dance and the two of us.

When the orchestra played its last number, I could hardly believe it was already one A.M., or how tired I suddenly was.

In the confusion of the day, I hadn't given much thought to where I'd spend the night, but it turned out Quinn did have a room at the Alvear, after all — he just hadn't checked in under his own name, which was why Graciela hadn't found him in her computer.

"So what name did you use?" I asked in the taxi, leaning sleepily against him.

"That also might fall into the 'what happens here, stays here' category," he said.

"Did they really let you register as James Bond?"

"I didn't even try. But Q. Fleming worked."

The lobby was hushed and nearly empty when we arrived, but the night porter retrieved my suitcase from the storage room where Manolo had left it for me. And while I was a bit worried about what all of my new friends at the hotel would think, not to mention various relatives, it seemed perfectly natural as well as a lot more economical to share Quinn's room. I mean, if he hadn't earned my trust by now, then nobody ever would.

And though it could have been awkward, it wasn't. By

two A.M. we were fast asleep on the king-sized bed, both fully clothed. It wasn't even awkward the next morning, though I did learn that Quinn likes to whistle in the shower. I couldn't tell what, exactly — not through the door and over the rush of water — but it sounded like something from *The Lion King*. This probably had more to do with Bea or Oliver than Quinn's own taste, and mostly I was surprised it wasn't the double-O seven theme music instead, but I still stashed it away in the "what happens here, stays here" file.

Just to be safe, we called down to the lobby before we left the room, and Manolo assured us he'd seen Hunter leave half an hour ago, right after he'd come on duty. Of course, he'd also been picked up by a car sent by the Brazilian Embassy, and that fact was a harsh reminder of everything Quinn and I hadn't discussed since our lunch the previous day. We'd stepped back into our regular lives again, and though that was a lot more problematic for Quinn than it was for me, he was every bit as determined to forge ahead with the plan we'd laid out. We checked and double-checked to make sure we had everything we needed and then headed out.

It was another beautiful day, sunny and mild and completely out of sync with our actual agenda — a hailstorm or typhoon would have been a more suitable backdrop for entrapping Thad and Samantha Arquero. Manolo had said the subway was the most efficient way to travel during rush hour, so we followed his directions to the nearest Subte station and took the train to

239

Avenida de Mayo. This was another broad, almost monumental boulevard, stretching from the Plaza de Mayo at one end to the Plaza del Congreso at the other, where the Argentinean parliament met in the Congreso Nacional.

We found Café Tortoni easily, with its name spelled out in stylized red letters on a white sign at the door and a tango academy above — I was quickly learning that there were as many tango places in Buenos Aires as there were hot dog carts in Manhattan. Inside, the space had the same old-world feel as the ballroom from the previous night, with a lot of dark wood and marble columns. The ceiling overhead was set with stained glass, and framed portraits and carved busts lined the walls.

According to both Manolo and our guidebook, Café Tortoni had been a meeting place for writers and artists and intellectuals for more than one hundred and fifty years. Now it was mostly for tourists, but that suited our purposes fine. It would make it easier for us to blend in when the evildoers arrived.

The room was beginning to fill, but we managed to find a table off to the side, where we'd be almost entirely hidden by a column. A convenient mirror on the wall let us watch the other tables and the entrance without facing directly into the room. And though I had the feeling that wearing one's hat indoors was an etiquette don't, Quinn kept his fedora on, as did I, with my hair pinned up securely underneath.

Now that we were back to reality, neither of us was particularly hungry, but we asked the waitress for *café con leche* and croissants so we wouldn't look out of place. And once she'd delivered our order, Quinn set his backpack on the table and began rummaging through it. He pulled out the pen that was actually a video recorder, and the bionic ear that looked like his own Bluetooth headset, and his iPod, and he fiddled around with them all for several minutes. Then, when he was satisfied that everything was ready to go, we settled in to wait.

Of course, it was still only half past ten — but we'd wanted to have everything set up in advance. And while that was probably wise, it left us with excess time on our hands to worry about how things could go wrong. I jiggled my foot in nervous anticipation. An hour from now, it was possible we'd have everything we needed to vanquish the evildoers for good. But I didn't even want to consider what might happen if our plan backfired.

"What if they don't show up?" I asked Quinn. "Maybe after yesterday afternoon they decided to change the time or go somewhere else."

"They have no way of knowing we heard they were meeting here this morning," said Quinn. "It should be fine." But I could tell he was anxious, too.

And all we could do was sit there and wait.

Except we didn't have to wait very long.

I don't know why we were surprised when we saw who walked in, just fifteen minutes after we did. But my breath caught, and Quinn visibly flinched.

"Great," said Quinn. "Just great."

Because it wasn't Thad, or Samantha Arquero.

It was Hunter Riley.

Thirty-two

I guess we'd thought Hunter would be busy all morning bribing Brazilian officials, but apparently not. And judging by the way he held up three fingers to the hostess, even though he was alone now, he planned on being joined by two others, and it seemed reasonable to assume his companions would be Samantha Arquero and Thad.

The hostess seated him several tables away, in a spot we couldn't have chosen better ourselves — that is, if we'd been choosing for Hunter to show up and thus dig himself further into his guilty hole. We were completely obscured by the column, but the mirror beside us provided a perfect view of his profile and the two empty seats at his table.

"Are you going to be okay?" I asked Quinn. He was holding his coffee cup so tightly his knuckles were white.

He shrugged, his expression even more grim than when he'd seen me kissing Manolo. "At least this should get rid of any final uncertainty."

Hunter hoisted his briefcase onto the seat next to him and unlatched it. I didn't see him take anything out or put anything

243

in, though, and a moment later he closed it again and set it on the floor. Then he took a phone from his jacket pocket.

"Unbelievable," said Quinn. "Usually he's on a BlackBerry, and that's a Pre. He must have a different phone for each identity."

Hunter didn't call anyone; he only scrolled through whatever messages had accumulated on the screen, occasionally taking a sip of his own *café con leche* or a bite of croissant. It was almost eerie to watch him. He was a lefty, like Quinn, and he was just as much of a fan of strawberry jam. The two of them looked so much alike and their mannerisms were so similar that, if it weren't for the gray in Hunter's hair and the lines around his eyes and mouth, it would be easy to mistake him for his son.

Either way, we now had the opportunity to check that everything worked. Quinn made some minor adjustments to his various gadgets and handed me one of the earbuds from his iPod, taking the other for himself.

And while Quinn might have issues with math, if Prescott offered a course in surveillance he would have passed with flying colors. The screen of his iPod displayed live video of his father and his table. The image was tiny, but the resolution was amazing, right down to the flake of croissant Hunter had dropped on one lapel. And though at first the sound from my single earbud was indistinct, as Quinn made another adjustment to one of his gadgets it zeroed in on Hunter's table, and I could hear every noise he made, from the clink of his cup against his saucer to the rustle of his napkin.

"This is amazing," I said. "And it's really all recording?"

"It's all recording," he confirmed.

A clock on the wall ticked on, and I felt myself growing increasingly tense as the hour hand approached eleven. It was strange to think that five thousand miles away, I was missing physics class. I wondered if Dr. Penske had handed back the results from Friday's quiz.

Then the hour hand was firmly at eleven, and the minute hand began creeping past twelve. Several tables away, Hunter glanced at his watch, and so did his image on Quinn's iPod.

A moment later, though, Samantha Arquero strolled through the door. Her driver from the airport was with her, but he lingered by the entrance as she consulted with the hostess and then followed her to Hunter's table. Today she was dressed in another crisp pantsuit — she must have had a person on staff whose only job was to press her clothing.

Hunter rose to greet her, and they did the New York double air kiss I'd learned from Patience. Even though it was twice as much kissing as the *porteño* version, it didn't have nearly as much warmth, and Thad walked in while they were finishing up. Actually, it would be more accurate to say he hobbled as he made his way to join them. Despite everything, I had to smile. He must have forgotten to stretch after yesterday's chase.

245

"What happened to you?" Samantha asked. There was a familiarity to her tone, as if they'd known each other for a while. And when Thad leaned in to kiss her, he went for the lips, though she quickly averted her head and he got the corner of one high cheekbone instead. He scowled, which did nothing to improve his appearance.

"Just a little stiff from my run yesterday," he said, and he sounded extra weasel-like, either because he was sore or because Samantha was giving him the cold shoulder. "Which you would have known if you'd bothered to return my calls."

Samantha didn't respond, and Thad turned to Hunter. "Thad Wilcox," he introduced himself. Then, in the mirror, I saw him pause. "You look familiar. Have we met before?"

"I don't think so," said Hunter as they shook hands. "I'm Hunter Riley."

Anyhow, they all sat themselves down and talked about the weather until the waitress delivered more coffees and left them alone.

Samantha glanced around. The café was noisy with conversation and clinking coffee cups, and only one of the tables directly adjacent to theirs was occupied, by a group of German college students who were speaking energetically in their native language. She seemed satisfied it was safe to talk without being overheard.

"Hunter, I appreciate your joining us, especially on such short notice," she said, her voice coolly professional. "And no need to worry about Thad. We've known each other for ages — we were even in the same social club at Princeton. He's fully up to speed on our project, so you can include him in anything you tell me."

"'Up to speed'?" repeated Thad. "I made your 'project' possible." And, yes, he did use air quotes around "up to speed" and "project." "If I hadn't tipped you off that T.K. was onto you, you would have been exposed before you got started."

"And without me you would never have gotten rid of your boss, and you definitely wouldn't be running TrueTech," snapped Samantha. "We both benefited."

"Most people don't have the luxury of sitting around waiting for their daddy to kick off so they can get a company handed to them on a silver platter," said Thad.

"I'm the brains of Arquero Energy, and you know it," said Samantha.

Hunter cleared his throat before they could get on too much of a roll. "I was just glad I could make it this morning," he said. "Working out the payments to the different regulators so they'll turn a blind eye to what's happening in Antarctica has kept me busy, and I know how eager you and your colleagues at EAROFO are for the drilling to begin. What's the status on that front? When do you think the wells will start producing?"

Samantha shot Thad a glare before answering. "The necessary equipment is on its way to the Ross Sea as we speak. Except there seems to be a minor complication."

"What sort of complication?" asked Hunter.

"A potential breach of confidentiality," she said. "You remember how we requested your assistance with the satellite photos a few weeks ago?"

"Sure. We arranged for doctored time stamps on images of the *Polar Star*, so that nobody could tell the ship never sank. And then we suggested to a few bloggers that it would be best for them not to continue their discussions of the matter."

"I know what we asked you to do. There's no need to keep repeating the details of everything back to me," Samantha said. Her tone was getting testy — I guessed Thad had annoyed her so much already that her cool facade was showing its cracks even when she spoke to Hunter. "But it wasn't enough. Who knows what the odds are —"

Thad interrupted. "A billion to one, by my calculations."

"Thank you, Thad," she said drily. "Against odds of a billion to one, it appears the threat from the two activists on the *Polar Star* has not been eliminated."

"They're alive, and they're somewhere in Buenos Aires," grumbled Thad. "And to make matters worse, the daughter's here, too, and she might not know everything, but she knows enough to be dangerous."

"What?" said Samantha. "The daughter's here? Why didn't you tell me sooner?"

"Why didn't you return my calls?" countered Thad.

"Because you can't seem to get it through your skull that I have no interest in a romantic relationship with you."

"That's not how you were acting when this all got started."

"The operative word would be 'acting,' Thad."

Hunter interrupted. "So, the activists are alive and in Buenos Aires?"

"Yes, T.K. Truesdale and the other one, the Australian. We haven't located them as yet, but we have confirmation they're here in the city," said Samantha. "And that's where you come in, Hunter."

"Oh?" he asked.

"We need you to help us tie up these loose ends," she said. "Do you understand?"

"I think so," said Hunter. "You're saying you want me to arrange for these people to be killed. Is that correct?"

Samantha took another look around, making doubly sure nobody was in earshot. "Precisely," she said.

249

Thirty-three

There's probably no good way to prepare yourself for watching your love interest's father plotting your mother's murder. I stole a glance at Quinn's face, but he was motionless, staring at the iPod's screen with his jaw clenched. Meanwhile, the conversation at the other table wasn't over.

"And let's not forget about the daughter," Thad was saying.

"I tried to eliminate the daughter in New York, but it was impossible," said Samantha. "Those absurd posters made her into a celebrity. Even when she was alone, she was being watched."

Okay. Maybe I should actually thank Dieter when I got home.

"Well, now the posters are here in Buenos Aires, and so is she," said Thad. "She's with her boyfriend, too."

Under normal circumstances, hearing that term used in reference to Quinn would have me doing a happy mental jig, but I barely noticed just then, though it gave Hunter pause. "Boyfriend?" he repeated.

"Seemed that way," said Thad.

"Do you have a name?" asked Hunter. "Or at least a description?"

Thad shrugged. "I only got a quick look. The most distinctive feature was his eyes. Even from a distance I could tell they were an unusual color. Sort of a greenish gray —" He cast around for a comparison, but I knew exactly how hard it was to find anything that would do justice to the color of Quinn's eyes. Thad's gaze landed back on Hunter. "You know, they weren't that different from your eyes. The point is, if we can find him, we should add him to that list."

Hunter cleared his throat again and set his coffee cup down. "I see. Well, it sounds like I'd better get moving, and sooner rather than later. If there's nothing else, then I'll excuse myself so I can begin making the necessary arrangements."

He was already pushing his chair back, and as he stood, his knee jostled the table. The cup he'd just set down teetered precariously on the table's edge, and they all reached to steady it at the same time. Of course, Hunter's cup turned out to be fine, but in the process Thad managed to sweep his own full cup to the floor, where it landed on Hunter's briefcase.

Hunter snatched up the case, and he might have thought he was swearing under his breath, but Quinn and I could hear him even if Samantha and Thad couldn't. All three of them were on their feet now, with Thad muttering apologies and Samantha waving a busboy over to ask for napkins. "It's okay," Hunter said.

251

Except it wasn't okay. The briefcase was starting to smoke.

Then it made a sort of crackling noise, like when a hair dryer overheats and shorts out.

"*Bombe!*" shrieked one of the German students.

And that's when all hell broke loose. The entire room erupted into a frenzy of screaming and clattering as customers and staff dived for cover, tipping over chairs and knocking over tables and bringing plates and china crashing to the floor.

"It's not a bomb," Hunter said, hugging the still-smoking briefcase to his chest. "Really. I'll just be going now."

Clutching the briefcase, he started moving toward the door. Not surprisingly, the few people who hadn't already hit the ground or taken shelter behind the bar backed away from him.

All except Samantha Arquero. She stepped into his path. "What do you have in there?" she asked, keeping her voice neutral and with a forced little laugh for the benefit of the spectators.

"Uh — you know, some papers and stuff — nothing important — I'll be in touch."

Samantha snapped her fingers over her head, two loud clicks, and suddenly her driver materialized by her side. "Where are you headed?" she said. "Why don't you let us drop you?"

The driver reached his hand into his jacket, and there was another click, softer this time, but familiar from TV and the movies. It was the noise of a gun being cocked.

And if all hell hadn't broken loose before, that's when it broke loose for real.

I hadn't even seen Quinn leave our table, but suddenly he rammed into the driver from behind, knocking him over. I rushed to help, but somebody grabbed my ankle from under one of the tables, nearly tripping me.

I caught myself right before I fell over, my ankle still held in a viselike grip. I threw one arm around a column to steady myself and tried to shake my ankle free. But as I twisted around for a better look, I saw it was Thad who had hold of me, and he wouldn't let go. At least, not at first.

His weasel face was twisted into a grimace as he grasped my ankle with both hands. But while my boots might not have been so practical for the occasional mini-marathon, a few swift kicks were all it took to break his hold. I might also have broken both of his wrists, but I wasn't going to waste any time feeling guilty about that. Not when Quinn was still wrestling with the driver — along with Hunter and some blond-haired guy who'd apparently decided to leap into the fray — and especially not while Samantha Arquero was quietly slinking toward the entrance.

I raced after her, skirting upended tables and chairs and broken crockery and skidding in a pool of spilled coffee. Out of the corner of my eye I could see a blur of motion from across the room — another woman moving in the same direction, her hair flying out behind her. We converged on Samantha Arquero right as she reached the door, slamming into her from either side.

The impact knocked the wind out of me and sent all three of us sprawling: Samantha Arquero headfirst into an umbrella stand and the other woman and I along the slippery floor until we slid to a stop a few feet away from each other.

I leaped up, readying myself for round two. But Samantha Arquero was lying on the floor, moaning softly, and she didn't seem interested in moving anytime soon.

"Good," I said, at the same moment the other woman said, "Excellent."

The voice was as familiar as my own, and so was the satisfied way she said "excellent," though she'd never, ever used it in reference to my science grades. I spun to face her.

The sensible bob had grown out to past her shoulders, and instead of a sweater set and loafers she was wearing a brightly colored dress and sandals, but otherwise she hadn't changed.

Then my mother was hugging me, and I was hugging her, and we were both crying and laughing at the same time.

Thirty-four

And that's how Charley and Rafe found us. They rushed in seconds later, followed by the Buenos Aires police and the local bomb squad — summoned by the café manager — and a bunch of guys in dark suits and mirrored sunglasses. They'd been summoned by Hunter.

"Look, they have the little wires in their collars," said Charley, gripping my arm in excitement. "They must be Secret Service."

She wasn't far off. They were from the U.S. Embassy.

Hunter hadn't had a bomb in his briefcase — only a recording device that hadn't appreciated being drenched in coffee. And he wasn't recording the meeting for evil reasons, either. There had been another reason for his behavior, one that had never occurred to us: He was part of an international task force investigating manipulation of the energy markets, and he'd been on his own ultrasecret mission to entrap Samantha Arquero — so ultrasecret he couldn't even tell his own wife.

"Libra," I said. "Carolina was right about that, too."

"What?" asked Charley. "And when did you talk to Carolina?"

"The scales of justice — that's a Libra thing, the same way the archer is a Sagittarius thing. And Carolina said Hunter was the Libra."

Meanwhile, Hunter hadn't been the only person besides Quinn and me making a bootleg that morning. We hadn't seen them, because they'd been behind their own column on the opposite side of the room, but T.K. and Mark had recorded everything as well, though T.K. had built her own surveillance equipment from spare parts while they'd been hiding out — that was the sort of thing my mother enjoyed doing when she had too much free time on her hands. And Mark was the blond guy who'd joined with Hunter and Quinn in beating Samantha Arquero's driver into submission. The Krav Maga had proved to be a definite plus.

So that was all good, and Charley wasn't even angry with me, either. Well, that wasn't completely true. She said she'd actually been absolutely furious, though once she'd calmed down she realized she'd have done the same thing if our roles had been reversed. And she'd done exactly that, hopping the first flight she could to Buenos Aires.

Which was why her phone kept going straight to voice mail — she'd been on a plane for most of the previous day. Then, when she arrived at midnight, not only did she make the same discovery I'd made about international cell phone coverage, she was detained at passport control.

It turned out putting Dieter on the terrorist watch list hadn't been such a great idea. Somehow our picture had been circulated along with Dieter's name, and the guy at immigration had thought he'd recognized me, but when he checked I wasn't in the system. He'd flagged my name, however, and when a second Truesdale arrived so soon after, an alarm had gone off.

"Have I mentioned I'm going to kill Dieter?" Charley said as we waited at the Café Tortoni for the police to finish talking to T.K. and Mark and Hunter. "I know he meant well in his own ridiculously insane way, but I was trapped at the airport all night trying to explain about mobilizing the power of the masses to the entire Argentinean civil service." Eventually she'd negotiated her release, and she and Rafe had managed to connect with each other and with Manolo, who'd told them where they could find us.

"Now, I don't know about you, but I'm starving, and as soon as we can get out of here, I'm thinking *dulce de leche*, which is some kind of caramely thing that comes in a variety of formats, including, most important, an ice cream format — I was reading about it in the in-flight magazine — and it would be a tragedy if we missed this opportunity to sample it for ourselves."

Between the recordings and the evidence Rafe found documenting how Samantha Arquero paid off Alejandro Frers using EAROFO funds, the authorities had everything they needed to indict both Samantha Arquero and Thad for conspiring to commit murder. It looked like they'd also be able to nail the EAROFO member companies for violations of international law. Not only would they have to call off their plans for drilling anywhere that wasn't strictly legal, they'd be slapped with hefty fines to be paid into a fund investing in renewable energy technologies.

We all stayed in Buenos Aires for a couple more days, being debriefed by Hunter and his task force, but then we headed back to New York. And the trip home was a lot more pleasant than the trip there. This was partly because Hunter had chartered a plane, so we traveled in style, and partly because all of the stress and worry and chaos swirling around me had finally been put to rest.

So on the flight Quinn and Hunter and Mark sat together in one cluster of seats, discussing how James Bond traditionally relied more on sophisticated mechanical devices than hand-to-hand combat skills to thwart his enemies, but Krav Maga might offer him a whole new way to get out of tough situations.

Charley and Rafe sat in another cluster of seats, and Charley did most of the talking there, about *dulce de leche* and where she planned to take T.K. shopping since being on the lam had left her with serious holes in her wardrobe and Dieter's inspired concept for a neo-Surrealist film featuring a private detective who could be modeled on Rafe. Rafe listened adoringly, stammering replies as required, which wasn't often since Charley's idea of heaven was eleven hours with a captive audience.

And I got to sit with my mother. Even now, after everything had time to sink in, it was sort of stunning to actually be there with her in person and not worrying that she might be dead or threatened or otherwise in danger.

"I tried to call you," she said. "As soon as we landed in Patagonia."

"I know — that's what started everything."

And I told her about how I somehow had just *sensed* the sixteen-second, static-filled message I'd received the day I started at Prescott could only be from her. Moments after I'd listened to the message I'd seen Quinn for the first time, and then I'd met Natalie, and Carolina and Rafe, and from there the knot had unraveled, leading us strand by strand to that morning at the Café Tortoni.

Of course, it took nearly the entire flight to get through the whole story, especially since we kept getting sidetracked.

"You're taking drama?" asked T.K., confused. "Aren't you supposed to be taking Computer Science as your elective?"

"It wouldn't fit into my schedule. And I know it won't help much on the SATs, but it's actually turned out to be sort of amazing. Everyone said Quinn and I were incredible in the scene we had to do from *Romeo and Juliet*, though that probably had more to do with Quinn than me."

And maybe the foreign travel she'd been doing really had broadened my mother's perspective, because instead of talking about how once we returned to Palo Alto we'd get my class schedule back in its proper order, she only said, "So, you're enjoying Prescott?"

I thought about that. "Enjoying" might not be exactly the right word, but it wasn't so far off. "I mean, I miss Erin and people like that, and I'm having problems with physics, but I'd have problems with physics anywhere and Natalie's been tutoring me, and then there's Quinn, which is huge, and even Gwyneth isn't so awful once you get to know her."

"And what about New York?" asked my mother. "You're probably not getting much surfing in."

I had surfed once, soon after I'd arrived, out in Southampton with Quinn, but it wasn't like at home, where I could be out on the water almost every weekend. "No," I admitted. "But there are a lot of other things to do. Quinn and I went to see an off-off-Broadway play, and Charley's always inviting me to art shows. New York is kind of wonderful, actually."

"Then why don't you finish up the semester there?" she suggested.

"What?" It hadn't occurred to me that was an option.

"You and Charley seem to get along well, and if she doesn't mind, I don't mind. It's only a few months, after all, and I'll be back and forth from Palo Alto, and you can come for Thanksgiving. Maybe Charley and her friend Rafe will want to join us. Quinn, too."

"You like him?" I asked.

She smiled. "What's not to like? Now, on a related topic,

how do you feel about Mark? Because there's a chance he might stick around for a while."

I'd never seen my mother blush before — not ever — but she was blushing now. And if that was Mark's doing, then I wasn't going to object.

We made it back to New York in time for Homecoming at Prescott. And Patience had been busy while we were gone. I wasn't sure how she'd done it, exactly — mostly I was just surprised Mr. Seton hadn't had a nervous breakdown when confronted with her full wrath — but everyone who'd been part of the poker thing had been reinstated after agreeing to do a bunch of community service and enroll in a Gamblers Anonymous program. And once Hunter spoke to him, Mr. Seton even apologized to Quinn and promised to write a glowing letter of recommendation to his first-choice college.

The Homecoming game itself was sort of strange. They played soccer, not football, which seemed un-American almost, but hardly any of the Manhattan private schools had varsity football teams. Even stranger was seeing T.K., Patience, and Charley together in the alumni section of the stands. T.K., whose closet at home was stocked entirely in sensible neutral colors, had on a red scalloped Rebecca Taylor top Charley had insisted would be too fabulous with her skin tone. Of course, when I saw her sitting between Charley in her orange beaded sweater dress and Patience in her Ralph Lauren weekend wear, I still suspected that at least one and possibly all of them had been switched at birth. Regardless, it was the first time since my father died that I'd had more than a single relative at a school event. And I had to admit, I liked it.

But what I liked most was the dance that night. I'd been right — Charley had wanted to find the perfect outfit, and this meant a silver silk dress from Betsey Johnson with a purple sash and full skirt, accessorized with tons of silver and pearl necklaces and sparkling silver pumps.

Natalie was there — with Edward, because once she'd analyzed her collection of data, running regressions and calculating confidence intervals, she'd realized Charley had a point — the most important thing was what she herself thought of him, and how he was with her, which turned out to be as smitten as Rafe was with Charley. Gwyneth was there, too, with some guy from Collegiate, and she even waved at me from across the dance floor. At least, it looked like a wave. She might have just had a wrist spasm.

And I was there with Quinn, who looked better in his suit and tie than any movie version of James Bond.

He might not have been Homecoming King material, but he was definitely leading man material. And at that moment, with all of the pieces of my life finally back in order, he was everything I could possibly want — the final piece to make the puzzle complete.

Now, if only the DJ would play a tango. . . .

Acknowledgments

With thanks to:
Aimee Friedman, Abby McAden, and everyone at Scholastic
Laura Langlie
Alex Aberg Cobo
Manuel Urrutia
Anne Coolidge Taylor
Michele Jaffe
Rulonna Neilson
Raj Seshadri
The Sturman Family
Wikipedia